# BRUTAL
# (Uncut)

## By Aiden Shaw

9   8   7   6   5   4   3   2   1

Digit on the right indicates the number of
this printing

Library of Congress Control Number: 2008923239

ISBN 978-0-7867-2062-0

Edited by Don Weise
Cover design by Scott Idleman
Interior design by Jan Greenberg
Typography: Eras, Melior, and Openhouse

Running Press Book Publishers
2300 Chestnut Street
Philadelphia, PA 19103-4371

Visit us on the web!
www.runningpress.com

# BRUTAL
# (Uncut)

By Aiden Shaw

RUNNING PRESS
Philadelphia • London

*This book is dedicated to*
*My Puddle*
*(Pedram Karimi)*

Acknowledgements:

Carl Stoddart, Daniele Minns, David Michael,
Donald Brady, Flora Evans, Greg Jones,
Joeseph Holztman, Ken Houser, Marc Wayland,
Mike Power, Nina Silvert, Patrick Merla,
Pepe Catalan, Rick Copeland, Uli Lenart, Yuk,
and my superb editor Don Weise.

# 1

I can't remember if the drugs were numbing my body or if I was still too high to know, let alone care. My mouth was open, and I lay with my face flat on a greasy carpet. A puddle of something sticky, sour and foul tasting had cooled against my lips, yet my mouth was dry. I must have been sick, but because I hadn't eaten for three days, all my stomach could muster was a fetid cocktail of vodka and bile. Slowly I stood, although it felt like melting, but upwards. My brain received distorted information from my senses and in turn, it sent out confused impulses to my motor skills. It appeared to be daytime, but had no idea as to *what* time, on *which* day, and hadn't a clue *where* I was.

Outside of the window was a drizzling mist. Through it, there was an unmistakable sprawl of run-down council flats, and I could only guess that I was in one too. Somehow I knew it was London, and from so high up I expected to see some familiar landmark. But I didn't recognize anything. *Shit! How far from home was I?*

Stuck in the walls around the window were syringes, lots of them. There was a doorway leading out of the room. I made my way towards it. Once there, I stumbled and was grateful for the support of the walls. My balance was fucked and uneven. In the first room I came to, there was a strong smell of dog. The room was empty except for a dressing table with some empty glass jars on it. There were some black garbage bags full of clothes on a cement floor, and a smear of what looked like blood all the way across one of the painfully bright yellow walls. Down the hall further, I came to another room, which looked even less inviting. There was a mattress on the floor surrounded by household trash with what looked like a person under the blankets. So, I went in.

*Who is that?* I thought and hesitated. *Fuck!* I was scared, but thought they might be able to help me. I pulled back the cover. A man lay there asleep, unconscious, or maybe even dead. There was something familiar about him, and some thoughts fitted together in a sloppy way to make a vague sketch of who I was with and where. *Why* I was there was far more complex. I felt a rip of disappointment and started to cry. The man seemed lifeless, but still I knelt down and tried to wake him. He didn't respond. I desperately needed some comfort, and so got into the bed beside him. His body was warm, so I assumed he was alive, but his t-shirt was damp with sweat and smelt of cigarettes. The man seemed repulsive, but I took hold of him anyway. By going through the motions of affection, I hoped to extract some sort of comfort.

After a short time of lying there, clinging to him, I gave up, rolled over and faced out into the room. That's when I noticed a pair of dirty old feet with cracked toenails poking out from behind a pile of clothes. I tried to focus my attention on them but realized that I was hallucinating. There was no way that someone could fit behind such a small heap. My body started to convulse. I wanted to call someone for help, a friend, but I didn't know how to go about it. This made me aware of how fucked up I was. In turn, this made me feel completely lost. I began to cry and lifted my hand to wipe my tears, but as I did

I noticed a bloody hole on top of the biggest vein on my arm. Where the red of it dried away, the pink of an angry infection took over. Instinctively I touched the sore and a weird sensation ran up my neck. Now, this wasn't my imagination playing tricks on me. It was very real. Luckily, I passed out.

This all happened early Tuesday morning after I'd been out clubbing and drugging since Thursday night, and the man's name on the mattress was Spud. Well, that was his nickname, because it rhymed — however imperfectly — with drug. Come to think of it I never knew his real name, but our relationship was only ever skin deep, or any hungry vein just beneath. Regardless, the fact that he had "too much" of whatever I wanted meant I hung out with him often. Although *I* wasn't always quite there, it seemed to be enough to satisfy him. Our sex was always intense, which is what I wanted when I was so high. Of course, it was probably only because I was that high that I wanted it. Sometimes drugs brought out the most unexpected things in me. That was until in time those things became familiar to me, and then predictable until I eventually bored myself. There were times I even disgusted myself. I let myself believe that I didn't recognize myself, and conveniently, I often wouldn't remember the things I did. Still, I continued taking as much as was on offer as often as I could. There were times when I was so high that I wasn't physically capable of doing any more drugs and couldn't even attempt to have sex. Possibly this was a blessing, but how would I have known?

I looked up at Sky, my therapist, and couldn't help laughing.

'This,' I said, 'Is why I have missed so many sessions.'

'That's okay,' she said with a warm smile.

'That's a kind response.'

'It's all I have for now. Remember, I don't know you very well.'

'That's also a kind response, I think.'

'You're not sure,' she said. 'That's understandable.'

'You're very easy on me, especially about my idiosyncrasies.'

'Is that how you see them?'

'I'm sure they're common, as in widespread, but they're not normal.'

'*Normal*. I don't consider *myself* normal,' she said the word *normal* as though it was an undesirable thing to be. In doing so, she made me feel better about myself.

Sky had a tint of red dye on her hair. She didn't dress up or down, neither scruffy nor prim. Her make-up was barely noticeable and she never smelt of perfume. These things only told me so much about Sky but they were never enough to come to a definitive conclusion about her. She remained enigmatic, which might well have been the image she wanted to project professionally.

After a moment of silence, I said, 'It's disrespectful of me not to turn up, and I didn't even call.'

'Do you think so?' she said, cleverly, making me both question my behavior, and account for it at the same time.

'Yes, I do.'

'Then why do you let it happen?' she asked.

'I don't know. Maybe I don't value you as much as I should.'

'Only time will tell you if you value me.'

'I guess so,' I said, putting my head down, genuinely feeling as near to shame as I was capable.

Even though it had been almost two months since my doctor had referred me to Sky, before today, I'd only turned up three times. When I did manage to get there she always made me feel as though she listened, conscientiously, but without making it seem like it was an effort for her. She was also able to make me feel as though she cared. Presumably, she was paid to make me feel at ease, but I couldn't help thinking that she liked me as well. I needed to believe this in order to carry on seeing her. When I heard her name, the first thing I thought was *I like that*. The second was, *I wonder why her parents called her that?* The third was, *I wondered if it's real, because it's so funny*. I decided that it must be real because it wouldn't be a name one would choose oneself, especially for a therapist, it would be too silly and pretentious. I wondered what her parents might have possibly wanted from a child called Sky. What were they saying about their own disappointments and dreams in life? As with every question I asked Sky, her answer was to look at why I had asked the question. So when I asked her about her name, she smiled and almost laughed, then suggested that I might want to learn more about her, as I might want to learn more about my mother. Her suggestions didn't always sound like they came straight off the pages of A Beginners Guide to Psychotherapy, but I didn't know it then and thought, *How clichéd. What am I doing here?* I'd already read about these theories as a teenager, when trying to find answers to cosmic questions like, "why was my acne so bad?"

When I asked Sky about the way she dressed, she wouldn't give me anything.

I'd always thought life was all about trying to demystify everything. I found I had nothing to grasp hold of. She didn't let on how educated she was, and gave no clues as to her social class, her sexuality, how she liked to spend her spare time, or where she came from. I had no idea who she did or didn't like. I had nothing to judge her by. It was important to me that she was "somebody" and so with the little information I could obtain from her I created my own details of her past, present, who and what she was, and where she came from both culturally, and geographically.

Sky's lack of being anything in particular helped us focus on me. My insecurities, doubts, and false or real self-perceptions had to be cared for like snowflakes. There were so many subjects that had to be covered on my Friday afternoon sessions in our very special little safe space in Ladbroke Grove. In those early days I would break down often. It was as though she was a witch speaking her incantations, and these had the power to reduce me to a mess of tears.

Today, when I left Sky I was sweating and shivering. My eyes were soaking wet, and my jaw painfully tight. *Whistle*! I thought, but when I tried it sounded too wobbly to recognize the tune that I'd intended. *Sing*! I thought in an attempt to try another tactic, but I'd no control over my breathing. It was no use, because I was at the will of my body, which was at the will of my mind. The trouble was that *I* and *my* were still so unknown to me, and as far as how it all fitted together, I was clueless. I trembled as I walked to meet my friend Ace. We'd planned to have lunch at the Lighthouse, which was a hospice/drop-in center for people with HIV and AIDS. Usually, there were patients sitting at tables. The food in the café was specially prepared for people with no appetite. It was high in fat, and both sweet and salty. Still, the patients just moved the food around on their plates. There was a garden, which despite its intention to be tranquil and sensually stimulating, was always empty. In the Lighthouse, there was always an air of something, or rather lots of things. Many people had spent their last days there and too many friends had walked out from it to carry on with their lives, unhappy and sometimes relieved. Personally, I carried my own little dramas of regrets and sadness into all the confusion, never unaware but always distracted.

When I arrived there I sat in the dining room and gradually, very slowly, became less anxious. Lunch there on Fridays had become a regular thing. Friends who knew I'd be there would sometimes arrange to meet me. Other times they'd just turn up and surprise me. I liked this, and loved them for it. It was nice for me to have something regular to do that wasn't drug-oriented.

After the session I'd had with Sky I didn't feel like eating. *Coffee!* Clearly I was nervous already, as my palms were sweating so much that I had to keep wiping them on my jeans. This caused darker blue areas to form where the denim got wet. *Embarrassing*! My head ached. It did nearly every day. *Painkillers.* I usually carried them with me. They were often the last resort, that is when out of coke, ecstasy, valium, opium, or heroin. It was possible that the man behind the till might have something that would help. *Here goes*!

'You wouldn't have any headache tablets would you? I know you're not supposed to, but . . .'

'How many?' he said, with innuendo in his voice.

'What's the suggested dose?'

'One or two tablets. . . . Every four hours, but no more. . . .'

I waited until he finished his performance.

'Three please,' I said smiling to counterbalance my fear of sounding strained.

'Three?' he said.

'I have this really bad pain in my neck.'

This man who worked the till had become used to me coming in and as he did, his attitude towards me seemed to change from friendly to lecherous. Where he had once greeted me with 'Hello', this had changed to 'Hello, sex-pot'. I'm sure it was meant to be friendly but when coming straight from therapy these tiny affirmations pierced my skin with a rush of response that didn't feel healthy.

Ace was already forty-three minutes late, and I sat waiting for him feeling self-conscious and alone. My arm was itching from the infection. It reminded me to take the antibiotics that I'd brought with me.

I would have left, that's if I could have faced the outside-world or even just one of its streets again, but this wasn't an option just yet. Then luckily he came skulking in looking like he'd just got out of bed, and not his own. He was in club-wear from the night before — stank of cigarettes and perfume, still high from whenever he'd taken his last whatever.

Ace was somebody I'd met about six years ago. I'd traveled up from Brighton — where I was at Art College — to spend the weekend in London. It was a Sunday night and I knew that if I wanted to get the train back the next morning I'd have to be up early. I went to a small pub/club called the Two Brewers. It wasn't central or interesting in any way but was near where I was staying. At the bar I bought a drink and then pretended to read the papers while standing in a good spot for all-round viewing. It hadn't been an interesting weekend so far and I was quite bored, and although I was horny, more than this I wanted some fun. There was a dance floor in the next room, but I thought I'd wait until it livened up a bit. First beer, second beer, third beer, each with a vodka chaser. I decided to go through to the other room, guessing that if I didn't do it soon I'd be too drunk to make it.

It was surprisingly full, and the muddy movements of the crowd seemed to absorb the flashing lights, so it felt darker than it was. The men all merged into one as though they were singularly a crowd. As I walked through them, somebody's twirling head caught the light then dodged out of sight. I wanted to see more, so found a spot to stand at the edge of the dance floor. A young man whooshed past me, and made his way from one end of the dance floor to the other seemingly oblivious to everybody else. He spun with his hands beside his face, looking so pretty and completely mad. He tossed and posed, kicked and shone in the dullness around him. When he noticed me watching he took it all up a notch. Now, it felt like the show was for me only, whereas before it seemed as though it was against everybody else in the room, possibly even the world. I could see anger, confusion, control, outrage, and such intelligence in his dancing. Whatever created it, he looked amazing. He was beautiful, and although I didn't fancy him, I was still attracted to him, so wanted to talk to him. There was no point trying to compete with him on his stage, so I waited and caught him as he came off. This wasn't difficult because he acted as though there was no other way apart from right beside me.

'Excuse me,' he said and fell into me.

I got hold of him by his arm, half helping him but pulling him towards me.

'You're a star,' I said close in his ear.

He stopped, pulled back his head and looked at me. Then, as though timing his response to the second, he kissed me on my lips, and shot off in the direction of the bar. Then suddenly he was back with a drink in either hand and offered one of them to me.

That night Ace came back to my place, which was actually the sewing/dressing room of Danielle's, a drag queen I knew. I didn't have sex with Ace, and I don't think it was for the more complex reason that developed later in my life. He swears that I said it was because he was too beautiful, and I don't doubt I might have told him that, but the truth was, I wanted him around, and lured him home with the possibility of having sex. This was one way I attracted people. Some might say that was manipulating, but if friendship was the goal, how wrong was it?

The next morning we had breakfast in a local café with Danielle. I planned to go into college late. Sometimes I would end up staying in London the whole week. Before we left the house, Ace picked up a lipstick and applied it as though it were the usual thing to do on a Monday morning. It looked so odd on him for he had no other make-up on, just a boyish angelic face, the blondest hair, pink cheeks and ears, then a bright red mouth that seemed to cover the whole bottom half of his face.

Now, sitting in the Lighthouse I felt both hate and love for Ace, and was still glad that he'd turned up. He was very twitchy and perched on the chair next to me, told me that he hadn't slept and wanted to go for a drink. This sounded like a good idea to me or at least an idea that meant I was distracted from myself and wouldn't have to be alone. We started on straight vodka and another weekend began.

# 2

**From the Lighthouse Ace and I went to pub after pub** getting more and more drunk. In the Compton Arms, I knocked over someone's drink, by accident. That was when we realized we were getting sloppy. There was only one thing for it. Speed. We headed for the toilet, into a cubicle, wiped off the seat and cut two big lines. Within fifteen minutes, our heads seemed clear and our noses runny. Now, with so much energy Ace wanted to go clubbing, but first he wanted me to meet someone. We walked a few blocks to a club in Leicester Square. When we got to the front of the venue all I could see were bouncers. Then I heard a squeal and the mob of black suits shuffled back to reveal a woman.

'You must be Paul,' she said, smiling, with a face that shone in a way that I wished mine would.

'And, you must be Josie,' I said and bowed. We both seemed over excited. The bouncers snorted, coughed and stepped side to side.

'Calm down boys, they're with me,' she said and showed us inside the club. I warmed to Josie immediately, and within minutes she and I were chatting like old friends, but we didn't have much time because Ace had a list of places to fit in that evening. He'd done his deed, introducing Josie and I. Soon after that evening I managed to see her again, by getting Ace to take me with him when he went to meet her next. It wasn't long before I had her telephone number and used it. I knew she always screened her calls, but for a moment — and only sometimes — in those early days I'd imagine her sitting around with friends and laughing, wishing she hadn't given me her number. This may have just been drug-induced paranoia.

One night about two weeks later, I was with her and a group of other friends. We'd been in a pub and had got quite high. At closing time, of course we didn't want to stop partying and decided to carry on to a nightclub. We all jumped in a cab, and prepared to charm our way in once there. But tonight the receptionist was a bitchy skinhead who wouldn't have any of it. He wore a t-shirt so tight that it looked as though he bought it in some kind of ballet shop. This was shocking enough, but was upstaged by a big yellow-headed zit on his chin.

'Problem!' he said.

'What's that,' I said laughing, assuming it was a joke.

'No Fish on Fridays.'

'Ew!' I said, '*Fish*? You're joking right?'

'Do I look funny?'

*Yes, I thought.* 'Depends what you mean by funny.'

'Now who's the funny one,' he said.

*Still you*, I thought, but said, 'I haven't heard that expression since the eighties.'

'Well, the eighties must be back, because it's strictly men only.'

'Come on,' I said.

'Read the flyer,' he said. Pointing like a bossy little girl. '"A sexy cruise crowd".'

'But she's cool.'

'I'm sure she is,' he said. 'But she's not what the crowd here would call "sexy".' I'd never heard the word *sexy* said in such an unsexy way before.

'Give us a break, mate.'

'I'm not your mate. We've crossed paths before.'

'*Damn*!' There would be no chance now, because we had some kind of history, apparently.

'Please?' I said, trying one final time, using a for-give-me voice.

'Back off Lady, or I'll ban you.'

At this, Josie invited us all back to her place. First, Ace went inside the club to pick up some Ecstasy, and then we got two cabs and headed for Notting Hill. I wasn't the kind of person who makes "new best friends" easily. As Ace said, I didn't suffer fools gladly. But already Josie seemed so special, and it felt good that she accepted me in her home.

Weeks rolled by in a continual blur of drugged acceptance, experimentation, and an unreasonable amount of expectancy. Maybe it was just anxiety that I confused for being something more profound. Sky suggested that I was abusing myself, which surprised me. I'd thought I was being hedonistic, having fun. Admittedly, it was an extreme way of treating myself, but I managed to justify it on an intellectual level, thinking I was learning by pushing myself to see how far I could go. *What will happen if I do this*? *Then this*? I knew it was hard on my body, brain, and emotions but I considered myself tough.

Most Saturday nights I wound up in Trade. It went on all night, attracting an excessive crowd, mostly gay with a sprinkling of transvestites, transsexuals and standard-assembly-line-drag, all completely drug-fucked. Although everyone was high, it was very serious. This included the dancing, the sexual energy back and forth, the talking, and even the laughter. Sex in the toilets was the norm, along with people taking drugs. Cocaine and speed didn't usually come in the more convenient tablet form, like Ecstasy, so there was nowhere else to do it. Some did use the toilets because they had the shits from their E and others just stood staring, thinking that any second some piss would come out. The more hardcore clubbers thought it inappropriate that such un-essential bodily functions took place in cubicles. But really it didn't matter how long anybody actually took since everyone in the queue would have lost all awareness of "real time", and were using their own drug influenced concepts of it.

Trade ended on Sunday afternoon and the crowd dispersed. They went on to either chill-outs — small house parties consisting of three or more people — sex parties — the same but naked — pubs — which usually had a drag act on — some took disco naps at home — all to reconvene at a Sunday all-nighter called *ff* back in exactly the same place where Trade had been. It always looked as though nobody had left. There was a rumor popular for a while that a dead body was discovered by a cleaner under the stairwell one Monday afternoon, and that they had been there since Saturday. Ace said that the sex change Lola — who was infamous for fucking her straight boyfriend under the stairs — would have noticed if there was something under her feet. Then added that her feet probably never touched the ground. If somebody had died, nobody knew who it was and so nobody had to care and the rumor fizzled out.

Everybody knew that both Trade and *ff* were pointless, if not unbearable, unless you were very high, not just regular high. My strategy for coping with both clubs was to start off by getting drunk to motivate myself, and then I took some E to make me friendly and nice, then I added some speed to the mix so that I could hold my facade together for a long period of time. Of course, if anyone offered me anything else, I took it. Coke was good for helping me care even less about myself, and it gave me a coke-specific-obnoxious-self-confidence. Acid colored it all in somewhat or at least rearranged it making me confused enough to find it interesting wherever I was. Alcohol would be a constant. If I found I was getting too high — which was usual — alcohol grounded me and if not high enough it made me reassuringly messy. It was a fine art getting the proper levels, but I became a master, mostly because it was something to do, a goal, instead of just being high in Trade or *ff*. Anyhow, I always carried a few prescription valium or Rohypnol for emergencies like, if I ended up somewhere I didn't want to be there. This happened for only two reasons; either I left my friends to go and have sex, then realized I was with a mistake, or if I began to ache from complete exhaustion. This wasn't just a head or muscular ache. It was more like every part of me was saying enough, my; organs, veins, skin, teeth and my joints. At this stage I tended to convulse and hallucinate even if I hadn't taken acid. I simply wouldn't be able to function properly anymore so had little choice. Just being had become too painful, and so I'd take another more useful drug to take a break.

One weekend I had peaked about twelve hours before and was nearing the painful stage when somebody gave me a different kind of cure-all. Spud the drug dealer took me to a house near Trade that belonged to a friend of his. He told me he had a treat for me that would make me feel well. I guessed that it wouldn't be reflexology, massage, acupuncture or an herbal remedy, but would more likely involve at least some class of narcotic being added to the stew that I'd become. Spud told me to sit and wait in a living room that was so untidy. It looked provincial, and tacky, so completely fascinating. Meanwhile there were kitchen noises of drawers, taps going on and off and then a gas flame on a cooker. After a few minutes I heard the gas go off, leaving silence. This was followed by his footsteps as he entered the room with a big grin on his face.

In his hand he held two syringes.

'This'll do the trick,' he said sounding cheeky.

'What is it?'

'Speed.'

'How do you know it's good stuff?'

'My dealer wouldn't give me shit. He knows I bang it up.'

'You could overdose.'

'Guess so, but I've been doing this a long time and I've never had a problem. I know what I'm doing you Silly Sod. Make a fist, and give me your arm.'

'What does it feel like?'

'You'll see. You won't be sorry.'

He tied a leather belt round the top of my arm so my veins stuck out clearly. I felt a prick and a slight burn as the needle went in. Then my blood seemed to warm and I felt a squirting sensation which gave me a funny dry feeling at the back of my throat. I lay back feeling calm, smiling, at peace with the world.

'Whoa!' I said slowly and softly. 'You're right. I'm not sorry.'

'Nice hey?'

'Fuuuuuck! How long will this last?'

'The rush will be over in a few minutes and you'll not feel like moving again, for a while.'

As he did his, I lay trying to fully experience the sensation as the speed pulsed through my body. Slowly I sat up, then stood and went to look in the mirror. I didn't appear to look that different; only my face had a freshness that wasn't there before, my eyes had a sparkle, and my cheeks had a healthier glow. It was as though three druggy, sleepless, vodka-drinking nights had washed away. After Spud stopped rushing, we hurried back to the club.

Now that I felt so fabulous, I talked to most everybody on the way down two flights of stairs, but rapidly. Then I sat by myself under a bright light being as conspicuous as possible. I had a newer more real confidence, and felt I could take on anybody or any situation especially as I knew everyone else in the club was flagging by this time of the morning.

From a quick scan of the wilting room, everybody looked as drug fucked as they always did but more tired than usual. Then a group of people came in the room that looked fresh, possibly having just arrived. I watched them to see their reactions to the rest of the people in the room, and in doing so I caught sight of a flash of pale skin. It was Josie. I shouted her name loudly. Everyone in the room turned round but more importantly so did she. That smile was there again. She left her company and came over. I couldn't have given her a warmer welcome. Through the noise, the bodies, the confusion and attitude it took just a smile and suddenly there was something real. It was such an unusual thing to see in the context of Trade. Especially, a smile that didn't looked screwed in place by Ecstasy. Josie and I sat together for what felt like hours and seemed to retract from the action. In time, we bent in towards each other and became very private.

A girl approached us seemingly unaware of our personal space and whatever etiquette we had just created for ourselves. She was wearing an unintentionally off-white bra, "hot" pants and had shoulder length perm-damaged hair, all of which were soaking with sweat.

'Hi, I'm Sara,' she said clawing at her hair and mashing it into a ponytail-like arrangement. 'Got any gum?' Josie shook her head. 'Have you?' she said to me.

'No.'

'Got any water?'

'Sorry,' said Josie. 'Only vodka.'

'Ugh! I don't know how you can drink that stuff.' Sara didn't seem to have any interest in me, but continued to speak at Josie, who listened, smiled and put up with her. This gave me my first chance to have a good look at my new friend. Josie looked so out of place in Trade where everybody — male or female, buff or frail — had taken their shirts off because of the heat. That wasn't Josie's style. She was cool in an elegant long-sleeve black dress that ended over a pair of Doctor Marten boots. A thin coating of pale foundation and possibly some clear lip balm was all the make-up I could see on her face but her shiny hair was dyed black and hung very straight. She was backlit by a burning candle that made her look like a character from a book of saints that was pushed in front of us every Sunday when growing up. I don't know if it was the drugs, which emphasized this, but the overall effect gave me a warm sensation in my gut. Unlike Sara who assaulted my vision with her relentless fidgeting, blowing air out of her cheeks, grinding her jaw and straightening her bra. Even after banging speed, she was exhausting to watch. I managed to look back at Josie who was delicate, strong and sure. She made me feel pure, safe and wholesome. Eventually, after what felt like far too long Sara left to continue on her quest for gum and water.

For some reason I told Josie about a friend of mine called Jess. Ordinarily I wouldn't have thought to talk about her in a club. Jess was from a different area of my life. I'd grown away from her, and was sad that I'd let this happen. It felt okay to share this with Josie, although I couldn't explain it properly. I think I was feeling it more than speaking it. Still Josie responded as though she understood, if only in that she realized that there was someone else who related to me on another level and about different things from what was around us in Trade.

Quite close to us was a beautiful Hispanic boy who sat at the top of a pyramid of other boys draped over a table and chairs. All of them were the stripped to their waists. All of them were sweating. All were silent. All dazed, but at the same time they all looked furtive and uneasy. It was early in the morning. The club would close soon and so if they were thinking anything at this stage, one of the main things would probably be who they were going to fuck with. The Hispanic boy who I'd casually had my eye on since I'd sat down, untangled himself from the rest of his pack and headed in my direction. I knew he was coming but didn't respond.

'Paul!'

'Henrique? I didn't realize it was you.'

'I was thinking who's that hot boy over there with that beautiful girl?' Henrique was a charmer and he knew I liked him for this. Josie smiled at him. I couldn't help smiling also. At that time of the morning, a compliment was always welcome whether drug-induced or not. I knew that he meant it to a certain extent because we'd had sex before with and even without drugs. We chatted briefly about nothing, and I told him I'd make sure to find him to say good-bye before I left. This was a tactic that most seemed to prefer, as it gave us both the option of possibly going home together, but without really committing. With Henrique I was sure to have great sex and be treated nicely. At the same time, I knew he wasn't exactly what I was looking for. As well as this, I wasn't sure yet whether Josie was the right person to come down off drugs with either. I looked at her and it was as if we both acknowledged the situation. Josie had been around gay men long enough to know that I would probably end up with Henrique.

'He looks lovely,' she said with a chipper tone to her voice. 'You should go home with him, there's no point in wasting your high.'

At that moment, Josie showed me that she understood my depths. She knew I was lonely and that she could probably offer me more than Henrique, but she was also aware that I needed affection from a man badly, and that I'd have sex to get it. From within it felt like I'd no choice. Although seemingly superficial, this was often how I dealt with my depths.

The term *depths* used in this way was something I'd picked up from Jess, and like so many things in life, once I'd learnt the language for my thoughts and feelings it helped me understand what they meant. Sometimes I talked with others just to see if they had more polished ideas than those that were, in my mind, still under construction. Sometimes older people had more fully formed ideas, but equally there were those who just seemed to have insight for no apparent reason. There seemed to be a connection between Josie and Jess. I wanted to keep hold of this. Jess was quite inaccessible, I could speak to her on the phone but I rarely went to visit her, yet it was during visits or when she wrote to me that ground was covered and we accessed our depths. Josie was at hand, I was glad of this.

When I got back to Henrique's place, we took some acid. I don't know if I slept but eventually it was time for me to leave. He was a flight attendant with Virgin Airlines and had to go to work. It was Sunday afternoon and I was going to head home but decided instead to go to a pub called the Vauxhall Tavern. It was open all day and also very druggy. I'd want nothing more from a pub on the Lord's Day. On entering, a "friend" gave more acid. It was sometimes the easiest drug to get so far into the weekend because it was so cheap and strong that nobody minded sharing it. Some other people that I used to hang out with bought me a few drinks. My stomach was still empty from the night before so it wasn't long before I was completely cunted.

Without caution or sense, I drank lots of Red Witch (a paralytic mix — from my teenage punk days — of cider, larger and Pernod). To any bartender who'd served me more than once, it was obvious I was on self-destruct. Added to my choice of brain-cell destroying alcohol was even more acid, and then even more. I lost track of what I'd taken, and within a few hours all my faculties also. Technically you can't overdose on acid, but I ended up lying outside on a grassy area behind the Vauxhall Tavern retching. I could no longer see, let alone walk or talk. The people with me thought this was funny and rolled around laughing beside me. A stranger came over, checked my pulse, pulled back my eyelids and realized I needed serious medical help.

Noise. Movement. Confusion. Now I'm in hospital. Nothing made sense to me, and everything I thought I saw seemed to morph and then implode into another deeper scary part of myself. I wailed. And I clung on to a hand. It was a nurse. The next terrifying eight hours were hellish, but slowly in a stammering way, things began to fit my usual concept of a world I not necessarily identified with, but at least recognized.

The nurses asked me difficult questions like the date and who was prime Minister, like ever knew or cared. Apparently they were trying to make sure I had my head together, but what kind of freak knew those things. All I knew was, I felt so fragile it felt a bit like they were terrorizing me. One of the male nurses gave me the money to get a cab home. I guess he felt sorry for me. Otherwise I didn't understand why he was so nice. He didn't ask for my telephone number or even flirt with me. Once I was home and my ordeal over I was annoyed that I'd missed *ff*.

My birthday fell on a bank holiday about a month later, and so I used this as an excuse to celebrate, which meant, go out and get really wasted. After Trade, Ace and I went home with some boys who lived together in a large flat in Piccadilly Circus. We partied all that Sunday, because we had plenty of coke. At the time I used to supply it to a handful of exclusive buyers. I would buy ounces, split it and sell it in grams. I never cheated them, just sold it at the going-rate. Still, this meant there was always some left for me in profit. Everyone was happy, including me. If that was what happiness was. But I knew no better. My dealer trusted me, he made a profit and I got wasted. The thing was, when you have a regular supply like this other things come your way easily. For example, if one weekend someone felt they really needed the coke buzz, and I offered it, they'd automatically become a "friend" for life. Then when they were flush, sometimes they'd remember and sort you out. This kind of bartering went on continually and sometimes sex became involved because drugs could always be used as incentive, so naturally a form of currency.

The problem was another, next day, happened. This was what people called Monday morning. And the coke ran out. Without hesitation or remorse we moved on to some very cheap speed with vodka to get the taste that seeped down the back of our throats. In reality, this meant that by lunchtime we were drunk as any Saturday night hooligan. It was no surprise that despite being high we began to feel rancid. Ace and I — who were one messy blob by now — decided to go. Even though we were really fucked-up we could still tell that the "party" we were at was *really* over. Ace and I'd somehow grown into a group of me, him, plus some scraggy "die-hards" from the Piccadilly flat. Now there were five of us. Apparently, we'd all met at Trade, and afterwards stuck together. By now, we'd all been together in one room acting like imbeciles for about twenty four-hours. Often on drugs a "bonding", takes place and it feels as though you understand your new "friends", like you emphasize with them. It usually gets to the point where you believe you are spiritually connected with these complete strangers. So, in this state, we all arrived back at my house and as I poured our first round of Vodka and some fruit flavored drink the telephone rang.

'Hey,' I said while silently making it clear that everybody should shut up.

'Hello, is that Rod?' said a voice.

'Yeah,' I said. 'That's right.' Admittedly, I had to think twice about my answer.

'I'd like to visit you,' said the man with determination in his voice.

'Have I seen you before?' I said, while trying to put a face to the voice.

'No, I got your number from one of the papers.'

I'd used the name Rod to advertise on-and-off for years now.

'When were you thinking of?' I asked.

'Now.'

'One second mate.' I covered the mouthpiece. 'Hey you lot. It's a punter. I can't do him now can I? I'm so fucked up.'

At this Ace rolled his eyes, and grinned.

'Course you can,' he said, with a wicked look on his face.

'What are you thinking?' I said.

'Oh just an idea.'

'Sorry mate,' I said to the punter. 'I'll just be a second.'

Again I covered the mouthpiece.

'We could get some more stuff,' Ace said in a whisper-like voice.

'How? We've got no money left.'

'We can pay for it tomorrow,' he said. 'With the money you earn.'

'Genius!' I said, and believed it too.

There was a coke dealer at the end of my street. Ace's plan was I run there, pick up the gear, free-base it before the customer got round and do him while still high. How bad could that be?

'Could you make it in an hour's time?'

'Splendid,' he said, as though tucking with greed into a delicious steak. I gave him the address. As Ace instructed, I picked up the coke. He produced the free-base activities. Then the others waited in the living room while I did the punter and even enjoyed it, I think. Although I couldn't remember what he looked like or what we did. Everything went to plan, and we even managed to time it so that we took some Rohypnol before hitting the pit of our comedown. Then we all slammed into sleep, hoping for the tranquil sleep of babies, only we weren't at peace, content, or happy.

# 3

If I'd hated anyone in my life up to that point, it would probably have been Josh. When we met, I was eighteen and was at a stage in my life where he'd had me to mold. He was twenty-six, to me an older man. I believed in him, and so when he told me I was clever or creative and could succeed at whatever I wanted, I felt strong. The trouble was this also had a negative side and when he rejected me, I felt pathetic and lame, not worth anything. This happened quite definitely one day. I'd hitchhiked from Manchester all the way down to his flat on a council estate in Brixton. We had already planned to live together, but I'd had to wait behind to finish an English literature class I was taking. One weekend

I decided to surprise him by turning up without telling him I was coming. When I arrived at his flat, all excited, there was an incredibly handsome man taking a bath. He wore nothing but a perfect American corn-fed smile. Josh introduced us. Brad held out a huge wet hand smiling and squinting as water was trickling down onto his thick eyelashes. I remember thinking how happy he looked in an exciting new country.

'This is my boyfriend,' Josh said enthusiastically. I couldn't speak. 'He's from Ohio.' I remember it so clearly. The words stuck in my head for life. Brad looked like everything I could ever have dreamt of wanting, with no possibility of being. I was only eighteen; I'd fuzz on my face, the puppy fat of a boy's body, skin too soft, lips too red and lashes too long for a man. How could I compete? At that point, standing in that claustrophobic bathroom, there was no room for anger towards him or jealousy. He overwhelmed me. I'd never felt more ugly or awkward in my life. I was too busy responding to react.

They sat and talked in the bedroom. I was told to sit in the living room. Josh eventually came through and said that I could spend the night if I wanted and that didn't mind. I did, so left. It was late, dark, and I was scared in a rough area with no real idea what to do. Somehow, I managed to get to the other side of London and hitched back to Manchester.

Josh was the first man to break my naïve heart, and as is often the case, the hurt never went away, I just got used to it, accepted it as part of me. So even though it was years later, when outside the Chelsea and Westminster hospital (C&W), someone called my name, and I turned around to see it was Josh, I was still shocked. He was out of context, out of time, and was barely recognizable as the man I'd looked up to, the same man who'd had me to mould, who now looked broken, with all life force gone from him.

The reason I was at the C&W was because the law had changed. The National Health could no longer prescribe Rohypnol, which were my sleeping tablets of choice. All this really meant to me was that it was more of a challenge to get them. Now I had to go through the rigmarole of booking an appointment with one of the resident psychiatrists at Chelsea and Westminster hospital (C&W) to get them. A mental health expert had to assess me to determine if I "needed" them. The day came and so I was walking by the C&W when I heard my name.

'Paul,' he'd said. 'I'm just getting out of here.' His head gestured towards the hospital.

'How are you?' It hit me instantly what was probably wrong with him and he seemed to want to tell me. I was getting more used to having this kind of conversation, so knew to let him lead.

'I've got cancer,' he said. 'They say it's in my bone-marrow?'

'Is it HIV-related?'

'Yes, but the chemo seems to have been really successful.' As he talked, it struck me how I was reacting, managing to have a conversation, showing little emotion, as if we were talking about a broken ankle. 'I've got to slow down and try to adjust to all this. I'm going to Thailand. I've never been. I should be able to get by okay on my sickness benefit. I'll see.'

'Josh. There's something I want to talk to you about.' I looked at the woman beside him, having barely registered her until now.

'Oh sorry, this is my social worker, Cathy.'

'Hey, Cathy.' I had to carry on despite her being there. 'Josh . . . I can't forgive you for the way you treated me.' He smirked in the way that he'd always done, making me feel ridiculous, stupid and wrong.

'If it's that important to you,' he said as though about to burst into laughter at any second. 'We can talk about it next time I see you.'

*Damn you* I thought. It was over seven years ago, but he still affected me so much.

'I'm seeing the psychologist here and I'll be late if I don't go in now. Can I call you?'

'Sure' he said and handed me a homemade, photocopied business card. 'You better call soon, because I'm going to Thailand.' It seemed as though by affirming this, it would happen.

'Bye, Josh. I'll call you tomorrow.'

Nervous and confused, I ran round the corner to the mental health department. The psychologist was running late and when she finally got round to me, I told her what had just happened, and cried for about twenty minutes while I tried to answer her questions. As I left, she reassured me that I would most likely be able to get Rohypnol, but that she'd have to contact my therapist first.

The next day and each one after that I called Josh, but couldn't get a reply. *Selfish bastard*, I thought. *He probably left for Thailand without thinking twice about our conversation.* About two weeks later I saw Brad in a pub. They'd finished years ago, but I knew they still saw a lot of each other.

'Tell Josh, he's such a fucking bastard for not calling me back.' From the look on Brad's face, I knew I'd just made a big mistake.

'Paul,' he said and paused. He half closed his eyes, looked away, back to me, then away again. 'Josh died.' He paused again. 'Last Thursday,' he sighed deeply. 'I tried to get hold of you.' So many ideas flashed through my mind, such as; anger, disappointment, betrayal, self-pity, and non-specific vulnerable thoughts.

I'd never liked crying in front of people, but Sky had created a space for me to do this, and so as I told her about Josh she passed me one tissue after another to dry my eyes. They all became soaked because my hands were wet with sweat as well.

'I stood listening to Josh,' I said, 'While he told me how sick he was. And I felt nothing.'

'You're not feeling *nothing* now, are you?' said Sky looking as though she felt my upset.

'No,' I answered looking into my lap. 'I guess not.'

'And you didn't feel *nothing* when you spoke to Josh did you?'

'No,' I said, feeling about six years old, but at the same time as though I were a wise philosopher making a great discovery.

'I think maybe you pretend to yourself that things like this have no impact.'

'Maybe,' I said, only it was so full of emotion I barely managed to voice it.

'I think we should look at this, because I believe it's kinder to allow ourselves a reaction.' I stopped crying and looked at her. She continued, 'If someone cuts you, do you bleed?'

*Of course, I do*, I thought. Whatever made me think otherwise? If anything, I had hemophilia; only I bled in distracting ways that disguised it from me and everybody else. This was one of the most important things I learnt from Sky; the impact things had on me, and the impact things I did had on others. What impact did drugs have on my body and brain? In addition, what kind of impression did customers leave on me when they treated me the way they did sexually? How did my lifestyle affect my mother? To my surprise, I realized that I'd never been aware of impact in my life. No wonder I constantly hurt myself, and people who cared for me.

As I left her that day, I met Josie on the street outside. She was on her way to meet me. We hugged.

'Your back's all sweaty,' she said, looking concerned, and I felt she meant it.

'It's just anxiety. I've just had a demanding session with Sky, that's all.' Josie looked into my eyes and could see that I'd been crying. She hugged me again and held me a little longer than usual. Then she linked her arm in mine as we walked towards the Lighthouse. While eating our lunch, I noticed that there was a memorial on. It was for someone I knew, but not very well. I made a half-hearted attempt at indifference then checked myself, remembering what Sky had said about impact.

Josh's funeral was about a week later. I went on my own because none of my current friends knew him. People from my past that I remembered not liking looked at me. Some did this through tears, while others managed it while expressing bitterness. Meanwhile, the memorial continued. Some men, who must have worked there, because I didn't recognize them, brought the coffin into the room. It was put on a conveyer belt that had rollers on it like they have in factories. After irrelevant words by a woman, there was a mechanical clanking sound, and then as though Josh had just kicked from inside, the coffin jerked and set off with an almost clockwork motion. It started to disappear between two flaps of stiff velvet-like material, which were pushed aside by the head of the coffin, slid along it, then fell together again as it trundled from view.

Wow! Was that it? Done! Had Josh slipped out the back way, through a cat-flap like exit? I almost missed his getaway. I was too busy thinking about my own thoughts, about how much I disliked the crematorium, everybody else there, and how kooky the whole event had been. I watched the tassels swishing. I felt annoyed. Couldn't there have been something to add emphasis to the last seconds while Josh's body was on the planet, besides the prattling from the pulpit. Josh was so pathetic to go this way. Yet, it seemed so apt that he'd do it like this, not making it nice for me, not bothered by what the show was like. It was such a disappointment, a complete let down, a non-event. To make matters worse the woman who had led the "service" stood at the only doorway waiting, and wanted to shake hands with everybody on the way out. I wanted to spit in her stupid hand, but reluctantly I did what I was supposed to do and shook it, in submission or rather, confusion.

The next day during my session with Sky, I told her all about it.

'Maybe you're confusing this,' she said. As usual, I sat there, desperate for her words, trying to fit everything in order. 'I would suggest that you were probably angry at the service, the way Josh was dealt with, how pathetic it made him seem, not angry with *him* at all.' Sky was using my words by putting them together in a way that made more sense. 'Maybe we should look at these things separately.'

'Why would I be angry at the way he was treated?' I said disgruntled.

'*Why* is a good question.'

'I think maybe you cared for Josh more than you admit.' She must have known this the moment I spoke about Josh and, as was her way, she had thought a great deal about it, watched my facial expressions and my body language, listened to the quality of my voice then pieced it together. 'I think you loved Josh and still do.

'I loved Josh?' I repeated with disbelief. Her words span through my mind and burst out in the form of tears. Sky made it all seem so simple although it was generally a tough journey getting there. No matter how slow I thought my brain was, how immature my emotions, or how sad I felt, it was always safe, because it was within the special environment that Sky had created for all my shit to be dealt with. At times, it was a cruel awakening and other times a homecoming. I'd think I was having inspirational ideas, but really, they'd come into my head because Sky she had fed them to me, and it was usually at their last stage of development. She'd allow me to do the final shaping and then out would come "my" discoveries. The funny thing was it always felt as though I'd known the answers

all the time. I think this was because they felt so
right. The way I see it is, I'd shattered and Sky simply said: Here, you forgot to pick up this piece of
puzzle and this. See now. It all fits together doesn't
it? In response, I the child would start to see the
picture being created and thank her.

I walked out from my session that day with the
newfound idea that I loved Josh. This meant so
much to me. Sky had sown a seed in that last hour
that held the beginnings of a life, one in which I
was capable of love and if that was true it might be
possible again. I set to work in my mind trying to
decipher the good feelings I'd felt for Josh. It was
early days though. I still hated him.

# 4

Cum squirted out my of pulsing dick. I'd only jerked off
out of boredom and wasn't even horny. My
thoughts were still on kissing and fucking with a
gardener I'd seen working in Saint James, when the
telephone rang.

I'd been sitting in the living room on a chair that
caught the afternoon sun. I'd only sat down to look
at the introduction to a new book I'd bought. My
plan was to save it for when I woke up the next
morning, as this was how I liked to wake to the day,
slowly, partly elsewhere still, and so not entirely
having to face my own world. As I sat the sun
warmed my crotch. In time my dick began to swell,
and before I knew it was pulsing as though begging

for my attention. And that's when I sorted it out. Just as I was wiping up the cum, my phone rang and I shuffled towards it with my trousers still round my ankles and my belt jangling on the floor. Cum dribbled down my stomach, through my pubic hair and back onto my dick. I cupped it with one hand whilst picking up the receiver with the other equally slimy hand.

'Hi. It's Ace

The phone slipped out of my hand and clanked to the ground. I picked it up again.

'Sorry Ace I've got cum all over my hands.'

'Oh, are you working?'

'No. Playing?'

'Listen.' Ace's voice changed as he guarded the receiver with his hand for privacy. 'I've just sold this . . .' his voice fell to a whisper ' . . . Punter, three grams of coke and he wants to have some fun.'

'So?'

'So . . . naturally, I thought of you.'

'What does he want?'

'Work it out Silly!'

'Sorry, I'm a bit post coital at the moment.'

'Well have a cigarette and leave the flat like any descent chap.'

'Ha ha. But seriously, what I'm trying to say is

I've just cum. I'm not going to be up to much. What does he like?'

'Being a bitchy-queeny-she-hag from what I can gather.'

'Good sales pitch.'

'No. He's lovely. A real sophisticate.'

'But seriously, what does he want?'

'Besides cocaine? I don't know. Hang on.'

Ace spoke to the punter over what sounded like a Weather program on a TV, and through this, I heard a stammering, lisping, effeminate slurr.

'Ace, tell 'im it's jus' vizzzzual,' said the punter.

'He said . . . '

'Yeah, I heard him. He sounds a real Prince Charming.'

'Hang on Paul,' said Ace as the punter continued. 'Okay mate. I'll tell him.

'I can't wait to hear this,' I said.

'He's got some gear he wants you to wear. Sorry Paul, hang on . . . Stan, I can't tell what you're say-ing.' More smudged-word-like-noises. 'Yeah, sure.'

'He sounds really fucked,' I said.

'That's your job.'

'Hey! I don't promise nothing. It's his job to get me hard and to make me want to do it. I take no responsibility.'

Ace lowered his voice again.

'I was only kidding. Don't think he'd notice if you did or didn't.'

'Are you dishing the size of my dick?'

'No. I'm sure it'd ordinarily be big enough even for Stan. But at the moment he doesn't know his ass from his elbow.'

'Great! I'll just give him the elbow.'

He has some gear he wants you to wear. I told him you're good fun and you like your coke. You will have some won't you?'

'Yeah sure,' I thought, it can't be that bad, getting high and dressing up. 'How much will he pay?'

'Hang on . . . Two fifty.'

'Okay. Give me the address. Does he want to talk to me?'

'No, he trusts me.'

'God he must be fucked up.'

'Or,' said Ace 'He just knows me well enough to trust me.'

'Ewe! How well?'

'Four or five grams once a month.'

I got a cab round and waited — for what I felt was too long — at the front door, before the door was answered. Stan was quite the spectacle, not your typical punter, as he was younger, quite effeminate and had an old school clone look about him. He invited me in, falling back against the wall, and when he collected himself said, 'Follow me.' Once he'd turned to stagger up the stairs I could see clearly the tight off-white jockstrap that cut into his flat butt.

The stairway led to a living room with a red carpet. The place was well lit, and made the carpet look very bright, almost throbbing. It seemed to pour over the top step on its way down the stairs. I glanced around the room, checking-out the place. Clear plastic podiums were spaced at intervals, around the edge of the room. On them were gold, black and white ceramic figures of muscular torsos. There was a single print on each wall, behind glass, and framed in bright-red plastic. I hadn't seen anything like them since the mid Eighties. They were all of women, wearing wide brimmed hats, and red lipstick. The first was smoking from a long cigarette holder; the second was wearing long black gloves, and was straightening her hat; the third was blowing a kiss over the palm of her hand; the fourth had long red nails, with her fingers laced together supporting her chin.

Stan explained, I think to justify why I was there, that he'd got sick of the scene and never got what he wanted. To me, he personified small town nightspots, where the highlight of the week would be sniffing amyl nitrate and "really letting go" on the dance floor. Next, with a mother's pride he took me on a tour of his home, tripping, stumbling, and holding door fames for support. The walls, and ceiling, in his bedroom covered in woodchip wallpaper painted over with black-gloss. Cupboard doors covering one wall, and a shelf the length of another, all got the same treatment. On the shelf, I could just make out a plastic figure of Jesus, beside what looked like a Bible. Black carpet started at the doorway, and had a chrome strip to cover the join. Several screws were missing, and it bulged in the middle. The door was stopped open by a brick. I presumed the whole floor was completely covered with this black carpet, but I could only see it in patches, through the bundles of, unwashed smelling clothes.

The bed was covered in sheets that had probably once been black, but over the years had faded to gray. From the ceiling hung the wire frame of a lampshade with a dusty red scarf draped over it. Beside this was a sling, directly over the bed, with chains too thin to really support anybody. From the doorway I could just see under the edge of the bed. There were several pillowcases, the same color as the ones on the bed, squashed at one end, apparently stuffed with more clothes. Maybe, these were the smelly ones, and the scattered ones were clean. I could also see, at the other end, spilling out into the room, a few superhero comics, a porn magazine, and a lone, stray cock-ring.

We moved on, back through the living room, and into the kitchen. Where the red carpet stopped, cream, patterned linoleum took over. This room clearly didn't have the same aesthetic as the other rooms, and I guessed it hadn't been decorated since he moved in. Maybe, he thought it didn't count. It had the obligatory gray/cream color scheme I'd seen worldwide. I think it wasn't actually meant to be a part of the tour, but was included so he could top up his drink. He got this from a selection of bottles beside a microwave. The fridge had three magnets on it: a Dalmatian; a glitter-covered pair of ruby slippers; and what looked like pink neon swirling handwriting. It was difficult to make out what it said, but I think it was the word *fabulous*. Tucked under this was a note that read *call mum*. There were cupboards, but they barely registered as distinct from the wall behind them, or anything else in the room. The handles were brass-looking disks, like a miniature version of a door-handle you might find in an old castle.

The nerve center of this room appeared to be a glass fruit-bowl area. In it were four brown bananas, small change, a comb, a stick of chewing gum, and a notebook. Behind this, propped up on the marbled, Formica counter, was a notice board covered in pictures of glamorous women, porn stars, and Polaroids of men (whom I guessed were previous prostitutes he'd hired), like mounted animal heads or trophies. Then Stan took hold of my arm, and led me back through the living room, into an adjoining bathroom.

'This is my favorite,' he said, and winked at me. 'If you know what I mean.'

'Sexy!' I said, hoping it didn't sound like a question. The wall tiles, carpet, towels, wicker wash-basket, and soap were all shades of black. In this room the only things not black were the red plastic marble-effect bath, and some off-white socks and underpants both with brown stains on them by the wash-basket.

'Check out the sexy ceiling,' he slurred. I looked up, seeing my reflection, and behind me, a hand with a glass in it. I smiled at myself, thinking the room a funny backdrop. 'We'll get in there later . . .'

he said, referring to the bath. I glanced over, and noticed several cigarette burns on it. I could not imagine how his reflection in the bath could be sexy. All I knew for sure was that I wouldn't be in the tableaux. ' . . . I'll soap you up.'

'That'll be great,' I said my eyes flicked to the soap; it was hanging from one faucet by a black piece of rope. Again, he took my arm, more to support him than to guide me. He pointed haphazardly to a chrome and glass coffee table. 'There's some coke there if you want it.'

'If it's Ace's,' I said, 'It'll be good.'

'I can't tell the difference anymore.' He carried on saying stuff, and I as I knelt down, I was distracted by a bowl of chocolates in colorful shiny wrapping on top of the table, then through the glass, at things under the table. There was an upside-down slipper with a foil milk bottle top stuck to the sole. Also there was some mail that hadn't been opened, and I noticed his name didn't correspond to the one on the mail.

'Don't worry there's plenty more,' he said, presumably thinking I was staring at the coke.

'Right!'

'Help yourself to chocolate too, and sit down.'

'Okay!'

'Let me get you a drink. Whiskey okay?'

'Sure!'

He went to the kitchen. Although I couldn't see a cat, the couch was covered in hairs. There was only a minute or two before he returned. The curtains were dark green, made from a synthetic velvet-like fabric. The TV was probably the biggest you could get, five years earlier. There were birthday cards on top. Most had cartoon characters, or beautiful naked men on them. It must be his birthday. I looked around for more evidence of this, but there wasn't any. The TV might have been the designated area for birthday. Every other surface was addressed with something; a figurine, a photo in a Perspex frame, a cuddly toy. He returned.

'So what did you have in mind,' I said, with innuendo in my voice, and the best sexy expression I could muster. He must have been anticipating my question, because he threw a black Adidas sports bag at my feet. Perhaps he thought things were moving too slowly. I opened the bag, and looked in.

'Help yourself,' he said nonchalantly. 'It might be easier if you empty it.'

'Where?'

'On the floor.'

I tipped the gear out onto the carpet, and started

sifting through it. It was mostly leather, rubber and metal, with an occasional dick-pump, or handkerchief. There was nothing surprising in the whole mess, but it looked dramatic against the red carpet, like props for a horror film. I sifted through it.

'Shall I put these trousers on?'

'No, they're mine. Look, the stripe's on the right side.'

There was a yellow stripe all the way down the leg. I reminded myself that this was going to be just visual.

'I like to be pissed on.'

'Yeah, I guessed. Shall I put this on?'

'No, that's a passive harness.'

'What would you like me to put on?' I said, aggravated, whilst still trying to appear sexy and cool.

'Try that cock ring on.' Big costume, I thought. 'And leave your boots on.' Could I look anymore ridiculous? 'Now walk around the room, he continued sounding like a king and I his servant.

'How's that?' I asked out of genuine curiosity.

'Lean against the wall, over there.' His imagination was at full speed now. 'Crouch down so your balls and dick hang between your legs.'

Thank god I was so high or I wouldn't even have been able to pretend to pull off this kind of act. I tried to imagine what he was thinking, which I thought could have been: *He's crap at this. What a waste of money.* Or possibly even *Wow what a sexy stud*! He had me crouched in front of the curtains which were held together with a nappy pin, and hemmed in a mismatched thread.

'I like that,' he said, referring to my facial expression. I must have been frowning. I was glad he couldn't tell why. 'I like that,' he said again before he went down for another line, as though it was going to intensify his excitement or take the whole affair to a different realm, which no doubt it would do, at least in his mind, being even higher. There have been a few times when I've been sober in a crowd whilst they're high and really very little happens. Things are said that everyone else who's high seems to connect with, as though there is something more happening on another level and there is. It's simply the drug level. Stan possibly believed he would release himself. Maybe he would just get sloppier, more incoherent, more demanding, less respectful, and generally not give a damn if he did. It didn't really matter to me because I was off somewhere too. A part of me was getting into the posing; and pretending to be hot; then another part of me was getting off on being able to think around what I was doing and how the drugs were affecting it all. My main concern became how I could consume as much of the coke on the table as possible. The whole event became a mess of him not being able to tell me what he wanted and me not being able to do what I thought he was trying to tell me to do. I think this went on for some time until I'd the idea of getting us into the bedroom, presumably to get him to cum so that I could go.

'Come in here,' I said, standing at the doorway.

'I like that,' he said again. 'Tell me what to do.' Then he squinted his eyes, presumably lost in some fantasy of his own creation. He collected his stuff; cigarettes, whiskey and poppers. 'I like that,' he said again. He scurried into the bedroom, and onto the bed. Ash dropped onto the sheet from the cigarette in his hand. I lay on top of him, focusing on the sheet. Like the couch, it too was coated with cat hair. I turned my head to the side, facing an ashtray full of cigarette butts. I turned the other way. Now, I faced a red plastic foldout chair with a cold cup of tea, or coffee on it. Mold floated on top. I closed my eyes and pretended I was somewhere else.

Then I came up with a plan. I knew the punter wouldn't want to be left alone, so I'd the idea of getting someone else to come round to take over so I could get out of there. At the time, I knew two lovers who worked individually as prostitutes. I fancied one of them and I got the impression the other fancied me. I phoned them and asked if the one who liked me wanted to work. I explained that the money was good and that the customer was relatively easy.

'If I were you I'd get him to take a sleeping tablet. He's got Temazepam beside his bed, and I know he has to get a flight tomorrow, so it shouldn't be too hard.' After this briefing, he decided he would come round. 'Can I have a quick word with your boyfriend?' I added just before he put the phone down. Then when he came on the phone, I explained to him that I was high and asked if I could pop round for a bit. He said I could.

When the other boy arrived I left Stan's flat, and because I was so high I forgot to get paid. For some reason, I asked Stan if I could borrow a rubber mask, which looked like something from a horror film. It had press-studs on it so that pieces could be attached to cover the mouth and eyes. It was actually a series of thick straps, which buckled at the back.

When I arrived at the boyfriend's flat, he noticed the mask sticking out of my jacket pocket and asked me to try it on. Once I did, there was no turning back. A bottle of poppers was produced and stuck against my nostril. Then while I was adjusting to the sensory abuse, he stripped off my clothes, laid me down and before I knew what was going on, he'd bound my hands to my feet and winched them up together like he was going to roast me. At this point — as fucked up as I was — I recognized that he was no beginner. Every now and then the strip of rubber covering my mouth would be removed and he'd try and stick his big dick through the hole. The space was in no way big enough, but he had animal determination. There was also a strap over my eyes, which I begged him to take off so I could see him — my assailant — but I wasn't allowed that pleasure. I was made to suffer in blindness. By propping up my head, he'd fed me poppers, continually. It felt as though my brain lost track of my body, and between them it got to the point where I couldn't tell whether I was upside down, inside out, or aware of anything that was happening to me. Strangely enough, I was still aware that there was something profoundly satisfying about it, more than just getting my rocks off. It was as though he freed me from the actual world and allowed me to float in some heavenly unfeeling womb.

I went to bed late that night, wiped of inclination to do anything else. I slept a Rohypnol sleep and had nightmares I couldn't wake out of, no matter how hard I tried. In the morning I got up in similar frame of mind as the one I'd gone to bed in. It hadn't been shaken off by sleep. I spent all day sitting and staring, getting up to make cups of tea, sitting down, then staring again. I thought about Ace and Stan and the sex I'd had afterwards. I consciously tried to hold on to these thoughts to talk about the following day.

'When someone wants to be abused,' Sky said, 'There can be an abusive tendency also.'

She had mentioned this before but I hadn't really understood it fully. She'd also suggested that within a relationship that involves abuse that the role is routinely swapped. One person may do something and the other feels wronged so reacts in an abusive way.

'Paul. Look at it this way. When you fantasize, let's say when you masturbate, if you imagine yourself being abused where is that other character coming from? How is it formed? How do you know how to be that character?'

'Wow!' I said. The idea never seemed clearer. Of course I'd had this kind of rage within me. *Shit*!

# 5

**During another blurry week, which followed who** knows how many like it, I woke late one afternoon still full of downers and feeling the effects of the alcohol from the night before. I lay, wrapped in my duvet instinctively dreading the thought of leaving its comfort, and having to start my day. As was often the case, the fact that I had to go to the toilet was the impetus for me to begrudgingly get out of bed. On the way to the bathroom, I noticed a letter had been delivered. I picked it up and instantly recognized Jess's handwriting. The postal stamp read Brighton, but it also had the date on it. How had four months had passed since Xmas?

Jess lived with a woman, Ursula. They were in their mid forties and had domesticated/artisan/religious oriented life in a house just off Brighton sea front. Although, their lives centered on their home, they were far from insular. They had the ability, possibly because of their charisma and intelligence, to draw into their little cottage style, semi-detached house in Ruby Street, all sorts of people, some bizarre, most extraordinary, along with Ace and I. They were able to seduce us, collect our life experiences and in a way feed on us. Don't think for one second that it wasn't symbiotic. I can't speak for everybody involved but when Ace and I were there it resembled a feeding frenzy. They were great value, and always supplied us with home cooked goodies like roast-chicken and chocolate cake. Perhaps they simply had a craving for stimulus, but what person doesn't? There are those who find it on television, some in the food they eat, and others find it by doing extreme sports. Many use alcohol or drugs to fill their quota, but Jess and Ursula seemed to almost crave intellectually brilliant, culturally diverse, sociologically extreme, anthropologically fresh, and philosophically profound ideas. In whatever way you want to name, or define it, their enthusiasm seemed limitless.

There were parts of their life that seemed obscured. I was only given shadowy sketches of their friends. I thought this might be because they thought I didn't have the patience for anything outside my here and now, the things at my arm, or dick's length. Perhaps they thought I'd be jealous. Their sex life was left a void to me and that was fine. These things didn't need to be a part of what they were to me.

Jess had an influential and protracted period as an academic. Her first degree was in theology at Oxford, her second in history of art at Sussex University, but now, with a humility I admired, she worked as a cleaner in Brighton HIV and Aids drop-in centre. Besides her education and paid work, her passion was painting, although using the word passion could give the wrong impression, because her way of working was measured, diligent, well thought-out and well-informed. I know this way of painting would be too tiresome, laborious, or uninspired/contrived for many more "artists", but I felt she aspired to comprehend, interpret and express the inner most subtleties of her soul, and she used her education, her intuition and her gut to bring all of herself out into the world and work it onto her canvases. The way I understood the method and execution of her work made me admire her and it, and probably influenced how I saw and perceived her paintings. To me it made sense that; in order to like a painting it would be useful to understand that it had a depth I could relate to, integrity, purpose, grounding, and that clear communication was the goal. Her figures acted as characters, her landscapes set context and her symbols gave a multitude of clues.

I'd met Jess when I was nineteen and attending Art College in Brighton. I used to always have lunch in a vegetarian café called Mildred's. A friend of mine who was in the year above me introduced us one day. From our first few words, she managed to reach into me. I felt excited that she actually listened to what I said, and more unusually she thought before she responded. The most rare thing about our communication was that she was honest, and I believed she meant the things she said. If I wasn't ready for this kind of communication, it might have been insignificant. That's if I hadn't been so desperate for somebody to access me, in the way only she was able. I felt revealed to her and discovered, in the way I was with Sky, and I knew that once she'd opened me she'd do no harm. Her intention seemed to be to both nurture me, and teach me more about myself. Jess had told me since then that she sees this as a role of hers, not in an unthinking resigned way, but as a proactive decision; knowing her strengths, willing to share them, to heal with them and even to love when needed. Fuck! I needed. This was a slow process, but when dealing with me she was persistent.

The letter in the post that morning read:

*Dearest Paul,*

*In our depths, you and I are one, but you are on a journey down a road that I can't follow. Your voice shakes and your hands sweat. Don't fret for I'm at the end of that road. Know that I will be waiting for you, my arms will be open, and until you arrive, I will truly miss you.*
*Love,*
*Jessica.*

What was I to understand from this letter? I knew it was true and I knew that no reply was needed or even expected. We were separated from where we had been linked. What she spoke of was where I wanted to be. The problem was, I didn't know how to get there, and I knew I would be sad until I did.

Jess was religious but not in a way that I found separatist or alienating. I'd been brought up

Roman Catholic, but after trying it on as a child, I concluded that any god that didn't accept me could fuck off because if they were all forgiving and had created all things, either they were lying, or stupid, or somebody was misinterpreting their word. Either way, it wasn't for me, because although I was sleazy, self oriented, and when coming down, an anti-social freak, at the same time I was also honest and treated people as best I could, so to my mind any "god" like being would have approved of me. When I first began to know Jess, I'd found her silly catholic god ridiculous, her use of biblical characters and events seemed hyper-fictional and irrelevant to me. It took around three years before I understood that she was using metaphors to explain her beliefs. Then once I felt I understood this notion, she took it a stage further.

'Why do you use metaphors?' I asked. 'Why not be literal?'

'What does literal mean?' said Jess. 'Language is literally interpretation of thought and feelings.'

I considered this. It seemed straightforward enough.

'I hear what you're saying,' I said, feeling a little patronizing. 'And I'm guessing I understand it, but it seems to me as though you're trying to make something real out of something that doesn't exist.'

'So don't you believe this stuff exists?'

'I understand it exists as emotions and thoughts.'

'But that's why I use metaphors,' said Jess, as she passed me a piece of homemade bread. 'It helps give shape to my inner self.' By now I'd begun to question, if not completely doubt my own argument.

'But they're still only metaphors. Surely you don't really believe in all that religious kitsch, dramatic, and gothic mumbo-jumbo?'

'Do you have to talk with your mouth full,' she said, smiling with such affection. 'The way I see it is, we happily believe that we can bend space time, or that everything is made of vibrating strings? Right?'

'Yeah, but that's science.'

Jess made a face imitating my stuffed cheeks. 'Squirrel, you don't have to store it, there's plenty more.' I rolled my eyes. 'This science you so confidently believe in seems equally abstract to me. They're both just metaphors or *ideas* if you prefer in this context, and we use them to interpret our experience,' Now she was being patronizing and had every right to be. 'These things seem real to us, simply because we believe they are. Belief suddenly become the key word here.'

'And?'

'And,' she said, with warmth and real love in her eyes. 'I believe in angels.'

'Um.'

'Angels like you,' she laughed. 'You silly sausage.'

'You could have said it like that to begin with.' Jess rolled her eyes in pretend disbelief. 'Do you have any chocolate?' We both laughed.

From this conversation onwards, she left me having to interpret everything she said, from her religious language to my own understanding of the world. The notion of language as interpretation wasn't a difficult concept, so this language barrier was crossed effectively, and furthermore, I loved our way of talking.

Something happened once, which made me realize the significance of our relationship and her way of communicating. Jess had been involved for some time with a French church just off Leicester Square and had become friends with a nun there named Sister Jane-Therese, after Saint Therese of Lisieux. I'd been introduced to her, and then whenever I'd see her round the West

End I would stop and speak to her. I didn't hide anything from her, so spoke freely about my life. I wasn't crude but I was honest. It turned out that weeks later, after one of our meetings, Jess had received a letter from Sister Jane-Therese saying: 'Paul makes me sad. Paul makes God sad.' To which Jess had replied in writing, 'Sister, *you* make God sad.' I'd been stood up for, justified in a way that only Jess could. Using her language, both this nun and I were able to understand what was being said. Who were we accountable to, if not ourselves and each other? '*You* make God sad.' This made me sad, but only because I thought this a rare understanding. Jess had become a star for me, both holy and intelligent.

My mother was very religious. We had begun having communication problems in my teens and although we loved each other, had never been able to get around this. This gave me an idea. It was likely that my mother might understand Jess' language too, and so I asked her to write a letter to my mother when I died. I wanted her to explain what I was all about and even why, if necessary. Jess would be able to translate my world, mission, and lifestyle in a language my mum would understand. She could be the voice, communication and link that I never had with my mother.

This was a challenge. My mum and I'd had a break-up about five years before. It happened when I'd gone to visit her. Naively, I'd felt comfortable telling her about my life, thinking I'd reached a stage where we could talk as adults, but I was wrong. There was too much she didn't want to hear.

'You're blaming me aren't you?' she said.

'Hang on, blaming you for what?'

'For being the way you are.'

'What, funny, clever, and cool?'

'No.'

'If anything I'm grateful to you.'

'Don't laugh in my face. '

'I'm not.' I said this with conviction. 'I like who and what I am.'

During that conversation and at the time generally, I thought I was happy, and I even believed it up until the moment I told Sky. Then from that time onwards, whenever Sky asked me about it, I'd cry. Every time.

'Why now?' my mum continued, 'Why are you telling me all this now? You have AIDS, don't you?'

'No, I don't think so.'

At this time, I hadn't. It was about three years later that I finally contracted HIV. Looking back, I think that this conversation was a lot for my mother to deal with. I was clueless what impact I was having on her. I just wanted to be truthful, and build some kind of intimacy between us, but that day I learnt that sometimes honesty isn't always the best policy. My mum slapped me across the face, ending our conversation. Outwardly my response was silence, but deep inside I said good-bye to her. From then on, I believed I no longer cared about her.

After all, how could I have known what it felt like for a mother to hear that her son was a prostitute, that he took drugs and risked his life? I would have had to have a heart, a soul, and at least half a mind, but ironically, I was my mother's creation, and still not kind enough to be sensitive, thoughtful and considerate.

Now things were different. If only in that I was aware how cold, hurtful and immature I'd been. At least I'd learnt something since that time; this was how sad I was about what our relationship had become, and you can really regret telling your mum some things. Deep down I truly loved her, and hoped that there might be a slim chance that things would be better if she understood me. I trusted that if anybody could explain/justify me, Jess would be the one, and she'd be able to do it in a way that would reach my mum, make her forgive me, love me, be proud of me and even feel stronger for what she had learnt. Jess was good at making *me* feel strong, and good about my thoughts, feelings and actions. So I could only assume she was good at doing this to others also.

I thought a lot about Jess' letter that I'd received through the post that week, and I wanted to talk to Sky about it. I decided to stay in on Thursday night, and go to bed early, so that I'd be able to get to Ladbroke Grove on time the next day. I didn't even drink, as I knew it would just snowball from there on if I did. While trying to sleep that evening, I felt uneasy. I'd start to fall asleep, and then cascade into a nightmare. Then, when I managed to wake myself out of it, I'd be too scared to allow myself to drift off again. The bedroom door seemed too open, and so eventually I had to get up and close it because I felt so vulnerable. After a couple of hours of my memory tormenting the delicate state of my mind not switched onto "fight", I took a Rohypnol. This barely softened the visuals in my head, and so half an hour later; impatient and pretty tired of being awake I took another two.

This was the remedy, I'm guessing, because next thing I knew my alarm clock was making a noise that terrified me nearly as much as much as my dreams had.

It was Friday. Eight o'clock in the morning. For several minutes I was confused, because I could hear a horrible noise and had no idea what it was. Then, as I woke slowly it dawned on me that it was my alarm clock. Eventually, I began to feel what I thought was anxiety in my gut. Then I realized that it was excitement. It was a similar feeling to staying up late when I was little. I couldn't remember the last time I'd been up at eight am without it being from the night before, I'd usually have been fucked up as hell, and would have avoided the light like a vampire.

This morning was very different. It was the heart of spring and I felt its heart and soul. I felt like Snow White as I opened my kitchen window and breathed in air loaded with scent. But suddenly I was full of confused emotions. I recognized a sense of loss, which had so often tried to creep up from within me. It had always been suppressed like the rest of my feelings, except, that is, when Sky allowed them free rein by drawing them from me.

The weather managed to touch something inside of me to do with a jumble of provocative, mixed, but clean memories: the first days of summer holidays from school, bonfire night, and fresh fallen snow. I decided to walk to Ladbroke Grove. It was a long walk but I felt up to it physically and mentally. Besides, I'd plenty of time. I headed down Earls Court road, and then on through Holland Park. There was a Narnian looking aisle of huge chestnut trees that lined the main pathway. The feelings I'd had when I opened the kitchen window returned, only more intense, and even more jumbled up. It was difficult to differentiate between strands of what I felt, but I sensed that some part of me loved everything around me; the smells, sounds, colors, and the very special combination of these things that was defining my experience. Over-excited and uncomfortable, my senses turned against me, making me nervous and wary. This flipped and turned into a feeling that something very special in life was missing. The last thing I recognized from within this whirl of emotive thought-like understanding was hate. This focused clearly on one specific thing. I was going to die of AIDS, that's if my lifestyle didn't get me first.

'Is this it?' I said to myself in a whisper. A little boy who was walking close enough to hear me, looked up at me. It seemed like he knew the answer — that it's all I was worth.' *Fuck that*! I thought. I didn't need to be judged by children on the street. Anybody in any gay club in the world could do that. My eyes started to water. The boy scampered away, and as though to take the piss out of my extreme self-indulgence a bird's song rose, pierced my ridiculous misery, and tore through my feelings with a surprising and intense love of all things. My mind toppled, with my thoughts in tow. Within my forty-minute walk to Sky's this cycle looped, but each time with a newer, greater self-consciousness than the time before. By the time I reached Sky, and the sanctuary of her room, I was exhausted, drained and numb. I tried to explain what felt like emotional assault I'd experienced on my way to her.

Sky sat listening, with the fingers of one hand covering her mouth. I'd learnt that this meant she was concerned, but also that she was working on some idea that would probably help my confusion. At first, with hesitation, she made a few false starts, pausing before any formed words came out of her mouth. If I was more knowledgeable about body

language I'd have been able to uses what her
actions meant, but I wasn't. Fortunately, considering my ignorance, she began to use traditional, easier to understand audio language.

'It seems to me as though you are waking to see
all these beautiful things, and you're stopping yourself because you're scared of what you might feel.'
She paused. 'Perhaps you're scared that you'll feel
too much.' I wanted to talk about the letter from
Jess, and didn't want to hear what she had to say
about that morning. Really, I'd only wanted to tell
her. It didn't seem important, just annoying. She
continued ' and I can't help being reminded of how
you stopped yourself feeling when you last spoke
to Josh.' at the same time, I knew what she said
made sense, but I wouldn't let it register. Maybe I
wasn't ready to hear it yet.

I don't remember what else, if anything, was covered that day. Sometimes I was so tightly shut that
even Sky couldn't get in. At least, that's what I
think was happening. I still had the letter from Jess
in my mind. I agreed with her that in our "depths"
we were the same, but what road was I heading
down that she couldn't follow? Did I really care?
Was it a choice of mine? Had I any idea where I
was, or what she was talking about?

Sky didn't deal directly with any of my questions. I guess it would've helped if I'd asked her any one of them. Still, somehow, she did seem to respond to my feelings. Indirectly she helped me by being with me, by sometimes being parts of me, and sometimes being my mum. That particular day she became the Jess with whom I hadn't lost a link. As she talked about my feeling too much for me to process, and my feelings towards Josh, or lack of them, and whatever else we brought to the table, I felt assured in her room, having the company of her, and it made me feel secure enough to decide that I wanted to see Jess, to talk properly. The next day called her.

I later learnt that there was a name for what happened that day. It was referred to as transference, the process of projecting people in your life onto your therapist, and in doing so you can dialogue with them and listen to them as they respond to you. This interested me less than the fact that I felt an inkling of harmony, in one area of my life at least. Even when I understood what was happening, I still used it. As time went by, the whole therapy process quickened. This meant I was able to link ideas by myself. She would sometimes smile in agreement or look confused as she pondered what I suggested. I felt I'd begun to understand how Sky's brain worked with what I told her and found I could relate to her way of looking at things, and correspond. Still, I was determined to remember that it was only *her* way of looking at things, as I didn't want to be consumed by her. I don't know why this was an issue, but it was.

# 6

'I didn't drink again last night,' I said, with more boyishness as the weeks passed. Another month had passed and along with it several Friday morning therapy sessions with Sky.

As was her way, Sky smiled, as if to say *I wouldn't think less of you if you had*. Her approval was important to me feigned or not.

'I still got drunk every other day of the week, but not last night.' If I didn't drink on Thursdays, then I managed to avoid taking drugs, got a good night's sleep and was able to get up in time. Naturally, regular sleep made me feel much more sane, although it was still nearly always chemically induced. I ate more and so even put on weight. As the weeks passed, I felt much healthier. Still, a day didn't pass without HIV bugging me. It didn't overwhelm me, but still it insidiously effected in everything I did. My "recreational" — by now there was barely anything leisurely or entertaining about it — drug taking was down to about once a week. Sometimes, I even went without for a couple of weeks at a time.

Somehow, without warning, Sky and I seemed to have been dropped in the middle of a conversation about my mum, again. As much as I tried to change the path of the conversation, it became clear that we were going nowhere else until the subject had been addressed. Outwardly I switched off and stared at my feet, but this tactic didn't work. Sky was too professional, sophisticated and knew me too well to let me get away with such immature decoys.

'You seem to feel uncomfortable talking about your mother.'

*That's right*, I thought, but said, 'Really?'

'Could you talk a little about this?'

*Let it drop, will you*? I snapped back at her, but only within my head. This time my response was to continue to stare at my feet, only now it was because I was confused. I'd felt uncomfortable. This was true, although I hadn't realized it until she pointed it out.

'What's there to say? She's just not a part of my life.' I knew my statement was weak and unconvincing, and I guessed it wouldn't suffice.

'Why do you think she isn't?'

'You know!'

Sky made a thinking face, which actually meant *tell me*. In all the time I'd seen Sky I'd never known her to forget a single thing I'd said. 'I told you about our argument before, didn't I?'

'Yes, you did.' She paused, I think more for me to keep up with where she was heading. 'How do you feel about that?'

'It's no big deal,' I said. 'Well, not now at least.'

'To me, it sounds like it was a big deal for you, and her.'

'Do you think?'

'Yes I do.'

'How do you *really* feel about it?'

'I don't care.'

'Are you saying you don't care about your mother, or the argument, or about your feelings now?'

'I don't know.'

'Let's stop and think about it for a moment.'

We both sat in silence until I was compelled to say something, as I felt she wasn't going to.

'I still can't forgive her for doing what she did.'

'Tell me again how you felt when she slapped you.'

'That . . . I disgusted her.'

'You? Or your way of life?'

'Doesn't it amount to the same thing?'

'No,' Sky said, pursing her lips and shaking her head. 'I don't think it does.'

'Surely, disgust is disgust.'

'Perhaps, but I think what you're saying is that you felt rejected?'

'I guess so.'

'So, you felt something then.'

'Yes,' I said. Yet, it was only now that I heard what I was actually saying. Somewhere inside, safe from self-examination, I'd known the answer, but I hadn't realized the significance of it. It was quite likely that I'd *always* felt something and probably still did. Thoughts surrounding my feelings around Josh seemed obviously connected too.

For now, this was as far as we got with this conversation/revelation, but it was easy enough to make me realize I'd been deluding myself, and I had to ask myself, to what end? If it was to protect myself from emotional pain, then it was still too early to tell, because all I could acknowledge was numbness, which I know isn't the same as acknowledging *feeling*.

With uncanny timing, I received a phone call from my sister Rose that same evening. She said she was on her way to the wedding anniversary of an old friend and asked if she could drop in and see me. My newly discovered old-news was still seeping into every other thought, and the only other thing I managed to consider was to avoid her. My brother had visited only a year earlier and after he'd left, I thought it was clear that he'd been sent down to see if I was well. I'm sure if I'd looked sick I'd have had the whole family on my case in seconds. I'd actually just got over amoebic dysentery and because of this, I'd been resting up for a week on anti-amoebic medicine, which if you drink while on them, you'd be violently sick. I'd lost weight but at least I was lucid. When he left, I could only guess I'd had the all clear, because I received no frantic phone calls.

Of course, I could have been paranoid, but I did know my family quite well, and my guess was that enough time had passed to warrant another health-lifestyle check on me. Rose arrived with her husband, to whom I was polite but not particularly friendly, and he seemed to watch me as I made and gave them both cups of Earl Grey tea. He said that it tasted of perfume. I was surprised he could recognize anything with the five huge spoons of sugar he told me to dose it with. Still he kept saying he preferred "normal" tea. I couldn't imagine he could taste anything but sweetness. After plying him with chocolate digestives to resuscitate his sophisticated palate, I tried my best to show interest in family matters. But perhaps sensing my arbitrary scattering of questions my sister intervened, and asked if I would go with her to the shop to get some cigarettes. Although I guessed what she was up to, I agreed, anything to avoid having to placate the husband any longer. As soon as we got out of the door she looked at me and said very casually as though it was a question about the weather, 'Why don't you visit?'

'You know why. I just don't feel like seeing mum.' I'd thought about this enough to feel confident of what I said.

'If it's because of the fight, don't you think it's about time?'

'About time what, that *she* said sorry? I just can't believe what she did to me. How can I forgive her?'

'Because she was upset. Because she loves you. Because she's from a different generation. How many reasons do you want?'

'I don't know,' I said feeling confused. 'And I don't care.'

As I said this, it didn't ring true, even to me. I thought of what Sky had told me about admitting impact and feelings. Rose and I walked to the shop in silence, bought cigarettes, headed back, and again timed to perfection, she stepped in front of me just before entering my flat. This was the last second outside the reality of the man inside who represented a kind of family life that I didn't relate to. She stood close to me, within my personal space and looked me straight in the eye, aware that with me of all people, this was her vantage point.

'Do you really not care?' she said. The slightest twitch of my face would have given everything away.

In an attempt to speak, I breathed in deeply, but instead of words coming out emotions rushed up and became lodged in my throat. Rose got what she wanted. I turned away, but she took hold of my chin, pulled it back to face her and kissed me on my nose.

'I love you, you Big Silly and so does mum.'

'I . . . know,' I said, partly in words, and partly in breathing noises and tears.

'Come on,' she said, putting her arm over my shoulder.

'Give me a minute. I'll follow you in.' I wanted to get my head together before her husband saw me.

Rose left about an hour later and I drank until I was just able to get out of the flat and into a cab. Then it wasn't long before I ended up in a dark corner of Trade vomiting. The club was doing its edgy thing, everybody in it was trying as usual to be sexy, macho, outrageous, or whatever their particular thing was. As always, the music was being relentless, fudgy, and bass-driven. And yes, even Lola was under the stairs with her boyfriend. Jesus! It seemed that even drugs wouldn't help me lie any longer. Everything around me was not enough, nowhere near and nothing like what I wanted any longer. Everything did however appear to be on a loop, the whole thing so predictable. I left.

I headed to Josie's, and once there, I moaned in the way only good friends let you get away with. For some reason I started to talk about Josh again. Then everything else seemed to come pouring out, stuff that had been upsetting me from my recent past and some way before. I went to her bathroom and realized that there was shit in my Calvins. I couldn't help laughing at myself for doing this. Josie found it funny too. Eventually, after I'd taken four Rohypnol, I fell asleep on the sofa with my head on her lap. When I woke up, Josie told me that I'd fallen asleep crying and that she had put my underpants and jeans in the washing machine. All I remember is that I was comfortable and Josie was kind. One minute it was Sunday morning, and the next it was evening. I don't know how I'd have managed without sleeping tablets. Sometimes the need to be asleep was so vital, I'd have done whatever it took to make this happen. Thankfully, their effect was often instant, especially if I took enough. I was once walking on my knees to turn off the television set and never made it. I woke up with my arm still reaching for the on-off button. It was as though I switched off and it didn't seem to have the rejuvenating affect of actual sleep.

Once, this happened when I was in the middle of fucking somebody while my dick was in his ass. In the morning, he'd gone. I can't help wondering how he must have felt, when he felt me slow down, then stop, and not start again. He must have had to push me off. I imagine it must have been difficult, as he lay on his stomach under someone heavy. How must he have felt as he dressed and left my flat? When I woke, I remembered that we had used a condom but there was no sign of it. The conclusion I came up with was that he had taken it off my dick and disposed of it somehow. I thought this showed he'd been well brought up. He's never spoken to me since.

It seemed as though I spent a lot of time crying in those days. These tears weren't all of the same quantity. More specifically, they weren't all the same quality. From my conversations with Sky I endeavored to categorize them into three types: One. *My life's a mess and nothing goes right for me* (These were probably the most self-indulgent). Two. *I can hardly believe such beautiful things exist* (These happened while watching movies and lovers finally got together, or good conquered evil). Three. *Pure emotion.* (These gushed out when Sky managed to make me *really* feel something). I enjoyed them all equally.

After taking drugs, I'd cry very easily. Actually this depended on the drug. The comedown from ecstasy usually hit on Tuesday or Wednesday. With more pure amphetamines like speed, the comedown would take longer and be more believable, so could hit you Thursday, Friday, or even Saturday. In which case you had to take more to cheer yourself up. I didn't know exactly why it happened, but I think it had something to do with depleted levels of serotonin. This didn't just happen to me, all my friends were aware of the comedown blues. Josie coined the crying as "chemical tears". They included all three of my tear groups, but were exaggerated.

'Why do we cry?' I said to Sky one day. 'Does it do serve a purpose?'

'We must have tear-ducts for a reason,' she replied.

I smiled at the simplicity of her answer. Then we both laughed. It did seem that simple. Surely, it served a purpose. Sky continued. 'You can cry from within the valley as you see what's all around you, or you can cry from the hilltop as you see what's below, aware that you're free of it all, yet it was a part of your life.' Now I felt I understood my tears, and this made me cry again.

During my sessions with Sky, it became clear that some subjects were more pressing. Drugs were an immediate issue and were being dealt with slowly.

I'd always taken drugs. During my time at secondary school, I drank Breaker's (the cheapest canned larger you could buy in England at the time) and got high on homegrown cannabis that my best mate punk-rocker-Brian-who-used-to-jerk-off-his-Alsatian-dog supplied. By the age of sixteen, seventeen, and eighteen while on a foundation course in Creative Art I was going to punky/alternative/gay clubs where they sold poppers. By the time I left home two years later, I added Do Do's — a bronchial medication that contained ephedrine (a substance used to make speed) — to my inventory. This fast became a weekly thing, along with lots of alcohol. I took a year out of drug taking when at college, but made up for it by very getting drunk. It was when I returned to London that I discovered ecstasy, acid, cocaine and more recently shooting up stuff.

Sky never actually said much about the drugs directly, but did suggest that I might be trying to numb myself and that more recently this may be specifically related to my HIV status. She suggested that I might also have a lot of guilt. Who knew why the process she used worked, but I started taking fewer drugs. Still, I constantly questioned the whole notion of psychotherapy, but at the same time, I reassured myself that there was probably no harm in it, although I wasn't even sure about this. I remember thinking that I should be cautious. I'm not sure if I thought I could be locked away as insane, or just scared that somebody could fuck not just with my ass and dick, but my mind also.

# 7

**Four years earlier, a punter/sugar-daddy flew me to New**
York to stay in his apartment on 64$^{th}$ street and
Central Park West. His name was Gregory. I'd never
liked the idea of sugar daddies, because I'd been
brought up not to lie. If I liked someone I wouldn't
want and definitely not expect them to pay me for
my time and if I didn't why would they possibly
want to. But Gregory was different. He was kind,
generous, extremely bright, and seemed to not mind
the power/economic dynamic between us. Who was
I to argue? We talked and he seemed genuinely interested in helping me. Gregory and I never had sex.

'When I see them marching every year, I don't
feel proud. Why do they behave like that?'

'It's only a bit of fun.'

'I don't see why they have to behave any different from normal people.'

'I guess it's because we've never been treated the same.'

'All that screaming and shouting.' Gregory had entered his own world by now and was neither listening or caring what I thought of what he was saying. This world must have been safer for him, more sympathetic.

'I think there's good reason to shout.'

'How will gays ever be accepted if they don't integrate?'

'*They,*' I thought, but felt there was something too fragile about his irritation to confront him.

He wanted children and I think he would have made a thoughtful father. He would happily have got married to do this. I don't think it would have been fair to any woman or to himself. As controlled as he could be, I guess for all his "good" intentions, someday something would have to give. To me, Gregory was only generous and kind, and I guess he got as near as he ever had to being honest about his true feelings. I could tell that he enjoyed giving me gifts and I being somewhat deprived enjoyed receiving them. Our weekends were spent shopping or sightseeing and in the evenings, we'd eat in smart Manhattan restaurants or go to the theatre. The fact that it was Xmas made it feel magical. Americans seemed to put so much energy into the holiday season, covering every branch of every tree with tiny lights, and giving gifts to each other to show they cared. This seemed particularly important to Gregory. I don't think his generosity was a substitute for kindness. We flew over the city in a helicopter, enjoying the wintry view together. The millions of glistening lights made me feel very special. I thought he cared about me, because he went to such lengths to show me. A more cynical person might say he was just exercising his part in a symbiotic control dynamic, and that in reality it was warped and unreal, let alone unfair, but really, what power could he have experienced in treating me — a kid in his early twenties — to sights, sounds, tastes and experiences that I'd never ordinarily have seen? Surely that was a sweet thing, despite any lust he might have had for me.

During the weekdays, Gregory went out early to work leaving me to spend the days however I wanted. I worked-out at the local YMCA, walked in Central Park, went to the little zoo there and discovered the cruising area. I was casually followed and finally spoken to by a man who took me back to his apartment, just one block up from where I was staying. He gave me acid and some Quaaludes. He ended up tying me up, pissing on me, slapping me and trying to stick his fist up my ass. Thinking about it the following week I decided that I'd enjoyed it, or rather, I'd gotten *something* from it, although I didn't know what. We kept in contact as he often visited London. Our relationship developed and became what he wanted, because he had a clearer vision than I did. He enjoyed dominating me. He made me drink his piss. He spat on me. He made me sit on his big dick, which hurt. He would position us in front of a mirror so that I'd have to watch myself be humiliated. He would put his dirty underwear in my mouth and call me his little whore. He knew that I mostly wanted this, but I think hr was also aware of another less worn down me, a soft boy who still had the same dreams of when I was a kid. This side of myself probably drove him on, when seeing that sparkle in my eye, and being aware that I still wanted love and affection expressed in a safe loving way. I always had the feeling that at any minute he might change, and stop hurting me. Maybe I was fooling myself, or maybe he was just good at fooling me. Whichever, well aware of what I really wanted, he would slap me hard around the face. If I moved away or even winced, he'd start to walk away.

'You shit,' he said. 'Why do I bother with you?'

I'd reach for him. 'Stop! Please.'

'Ah, you want me to stay. You like what I do to you, don't you?'

Then he'd start hitting me until I answered.

'Yes.' Now that I was tamed, instantly he changed. 'My baby's hurt. I'll be good to you but you've go to behave.'

This must have been what I waited for because it felt tender, real and felt like love.

Mark gave me my first taste of this kind of sex, and now along with my new wave of drug taking this violent/aggressive sex tendency expressed itself again, where sometimes I was restrained and physically violated or just psychologically degraded. This also seeped into my nonsexual relationships; hurting/being hurt, controlling/being controlled, and playing out roles/acting-out. Although it was much more noticeable within my sex-life and exaggerated when on drugs. This was where Sky and I began our work. It was directly linked with drugs because taking them facilitated the outlet. She suggested that taking drugs to begin with was just another means of self-abuse.

# 8

**Everything had changed. Gregory came to London and** arranged to meet me in the restaurant at the Savoy. He told me that I hadn't taken responsibility for my actions and because of this, he'd fallen in love with me. As far as he was concerned, prostitution had made me too callous to notice I was hurting him. What he hadn't realized was that I knew he was fooling himself to a certain degree, but thought he had the intelligence to know what was going on between us. I didn't feel I was to blame. He was looking for love in an odd place. Obviously, it wasn't a love affair. Could love possibly grow within this? As a rule, Gregory didn't like gay people. He wanted a wife and a family. Did he not consider the unlikelihood of getting what he wanted when he looked for it in a male whore, who was at least twenty years younger than him? Then when he did finally realize that he wasn't getting what he wanted, was he so surprised? Perhaps he really believed that if he spent enough money on me, in time I'd have fallen in love with him. I found this hard to believe, because even *I* knew that it just doesn't happen like that. It's a shame because he was a nice man — if not a little mixed up — and I could have grown to love him as a friend, but this probably wouldn't have been enough. Therefore, the finger was pointed at me, and I was evil personified. He must have felt so just in accusing me of impropriety and not being honest. I felt like shouting wake up Gregory! I'm a prostitute. I have sex with people because they give me money not because I love them. Sparks of spittle shot from his mouth as he attempted to crush my ego and will. Throughout his tirade we were served politely course after course of delicious food. I sat patiently. We finished with jam and clotted cream filled scones. Although I found my dinner date ridiculous and deluded, I couldn't help but enjoy the lovely food. The whole event took about two and a half hours. Finally I left, feeling good about myself with a satisfied tummy.

Prostitution, as you might expect, featured highly during my sessions with Sky. It was complex and seemed to be linked to everything I did in life. A lot of Sky's work was about helping me to link fragmented parts of my life, which I had a tendency to separate. These were things like sex and emotion, cause and expression of anger, even reality and fantasy.

I always like to use the word *prostitution* for the work I did, although many words were used. For me, *Rent-boy* seemed to conjure up images of teenagers on the street who'd run away from home. I'd worked on the street but anyone who had any sense could get it together to put out an ad so they wouldn't have to stand around susceptible to shitty weather, thugs, or the police. The word *hooker* reminded me of leggy, skimpily dressed American women from TV detective shows. *Hustler* was the one I really disliked, because it implied anyone who did the work would steal from you, mug you, or generally rip you off. This seemed so far from the truth as I can't remember how many times punters have tried to mistreat me or get away without paying. When people used the terms *escort* and *masseur* I always felt sorry for them; using use such euphemisms to help themselves own the work they do. Lastly, the anthropological definition *sex work-*

*er* reminds me that there are socially minded people in the world, but I find it a bit patronizing. I
don't need validating, and so they can keep their
political correctness for somebody who needs it. I
feel that the word *prostitute* says: 'Do you have a
problem with that?' Thinking about it, that sounds
somewhat hostile. If *I* hadn't a problem with it, why
would I be so confrontational? One thing I'm sure
of it this; my mother didn't like any of the words
anybody used, but I think I can safely say that this
was more about not liking me doing the work.

Don't get me wrong, it's not as though I didn't
have a problem with aspects of prostitution, just
not the "immorality" associated with it. I've been
told so often that it's fucked with my head and
heart I'm finally inclined to believe it. Apparently,
it disconnects emotion and sex. If this were true, I'd
have to ask myself: Did prostitution create the disconnection, or was I already disconnected? If I was,
that made prostitution ideal for me. Sky suggested
that it was almost certainly a bit of both and
whichever it was, the disconnection is likely to
have been compounded by the work. She seemed
on target with this idea, but it left me wondering,
why wasn't I complete/together to begin with? I
think sex work probably had different effects on

each individual. People often asked me if it got confusing. How could I tell the difference between sex
with punters and sex for fun? My response was to
ask them to imagine what it would feel like to have
sex with thousands of men whom they found repulsive, and then afterwards how different it would
feel to have one person touch them who they liked.
If anything, it clarified things in that department at
least. I joked that it would be great not being able to
tell the difference and be paid for having fun. After
working as a prostitute for so many years, I noticed
that I had to be turned on to someone mentally
more than I used to. I'd swoon if a man said the
right thing to me. This could have ranged from . . .
'I can't wait to see you, kiss you and hold you,'
through to . . . 'Lick my ass and shut the fuck up.' It
was about empathy, and showing an understanding
of intensity. I'd get off on the fact that my partner
might be bright enough to understand and then be
bothered enough to show it. In an odd kind of way,
it would show that they cared. Good looks didn't
do much for me. On the other hand, I've found having sex with ugly men exciting. This is because it
feels self-abasing. I'll explain: as a prostitute, I have
been continually worshipped physically, and so on
one level I like degradation purely because it's dif-

ferent. The oddest thing is men don't seem to like doing it if they know you like it. Otherwise they're usually more than happy to be abusive.

I met an alcoholic once who suggested that prostitution had made me lose my self-respect. He had come across this idea as part of the twelve-step program he was offered at AA. I slowly began to relate to this, not realizing that it might not be relevant. Eventually, I interpreted a great deal of my thoughts and feelings to fit in with what he had said. It was only as my drug and alcohol habits eased, that I realized that my insecurities may have been related to chemical addiction and not prostitution at all. I'd hate to think that I'd made a mistake all these years and prostitution had really fucked me up. I knew that it had brought about changes in my life but I found the changes interesting. I'd like to believe prostitution a valid occupation whatever the general morality on the subject is. In relation to what the law dictates, as far as I'm concerned, it has proved itself insensitive, unjust and entirely wrong about too many things. How could I begin to respect it?

# 9

Autumn arrived and like many pink blooded, hard acting, softhearted men, I had fantasies of cuddling up in bed with somebody lovely. In my dream, I spent the whole day in bed, under the covers, while rubbing my cold nose against his warm lips, snug from the heat of him and avoiding the chill of reality. It was in this frame of mind that I noticed a man in the bar I was in after coming from the gym. I watched him for a while and liked the way he stood with his legs apart, interacted with the people around him, blinked before he went to say something, and more than occasionally looked over at me while still facing the person he was talking to. Then he appeared to head towards the toilet. I thought to somehow cut him off on his way back. Unfortunately, a crowd of my friends came in and I was distracted enough not to see where he went. Regardless, I decided to attempt to follow him and possibly try to make first contact, beyond the communication we'd been having for the last three quarters of an hour. I turned and he was right behind me.

'Oh, sorry,' he said. 'I didn't realize you were with friends.'

'I'm not. . . . I mean they're not my friends. What I mean is. . . . I hadn't planned to meet them.' We both laughed at my clumsy explanation. 'I'd rather talk to you is what I'm trying to say.'

'Cool,' he said.

'They'll understand if they're any friends at all.'

At this point, I was handed a drink and sure enough, my friends left me alone.

'Considerate friends,' he said.

'Yeah, or just well trained.'

'It's good either way.'

'Right! What's your name?'

'Joel.'

This is how the conversation went. Clearly, it was nothing special, but it was nice all the same. We arranged to meet for a date — not a "hook up" — over the weekend and went to see a film. I felt as though he liked me, and — for no better reasons than indoctrination since birth, and an unhealthy amount of desperation — already I had expectations. He asked if we could get together again and so I told him I'd call. Despite the fact I'd been thinking about him the whole next day, I waited until the evening to call so as not to seem to keen.

'Hey, Joel.'

'How you doing?'

'Good, it was nice hanging you with you last night.'

'Yeah you too.'

'I'd love to get together again,' I said, genuinely quite excited.

'Great!'

'If you're not doing anything this weekend, you could come over to my place and I'll cook us something.'

'Hmmm! I don't know.'

'Don't worry, I'm quite a good cook, and I promise it'll be low fat.'

'I'd rather *you* came over *here*,' he said. I paused a moment wondering why he was reticent. 'If you don't mind.'

'No.' I said. 'I mean, no I don't mind. Sure, that's cool.'

'It's just that I was telling my boyfriend about you and he said to ask you if you'd come round here for dinner.'

'Boyfriend?' I said. *Fuck. Fuck. Fuck*, I thought.

'Yeah, he's a chef. You won't be disappointed. If you know what I mean.'

'What's he like?' I said. *Fuck. Fuck. Fuck*, I thought.

'It's German Jason. You know him.'

'Jason?' I said, still reeling from the shock, and not being able to focus on recalling faces.

'You spoke to him at *ff* a few weeks ago and you planned to go home with him.' This didn't narrow it down much.

'My memory's not great when I'm high.'

'You were all over each other.' Again, this could have been one of a number of people.

'Jason?' I repeated, as I tried to compose my feelings.

'Really defined, short, wears glasses. Anyway, he knows you.'

Then suddenly it came to me. I'd always had a soft spot for a man in glasses, especially in clubs.

'Oh, right. Yeah. I do remember. He's your boyfriend is he? Wow! What a coincidence.' The annoying thing was, I did want to fuck with him.

'He's a horny bugger.'

'You're telling me! Anyway, would you be into it?'

'I'm not sure.'

'I promise you, we'll treat you real good.'

I interpreted this as, we're going to sandwich you. I'd known from experience that with boyfriends, one tended to like fucking and one getting fucked, so in a three-way situation the newcomer was often in the middle. Tough decision. Should I fuck a horny man, while being fucked by another? Why did life throw such hard decisions at me?

'I don't know. Are you sure you're both cool about it?' What I meant by this was, had they done it before and did it work out okay. I had experienced situations where one would get jealous if I spent too much time with the other. Then I'd have to concentrate more on the one feeling left out. On drugs, sometimes the only fucking that went on was with my head. It'd get so confusing and I'd end up having sex more with the one I didn't like as much. Also, out of insecurity sometimes they'd start being really loving with each other, which meant; your services are no longer required. On the other hand, if it went well it could be fulfilling in more than a couple of ways.

'Yeah, we both think you're cute. It'll be hot.'

'Okay. When?'

So, we arranged the date, although deep down I felt unsure, them not being able to handle it obviously wasn't the only problem.

Despite my apprehension, it couldn't have gone better. The warm — but at the same time very sexy — welcome; the foreplay, which kept my interest so much I wasn't waiting for the fucking to begin; then just as expected — but the best I'd ever tasted — sandwich; and to round the evening off perfectly, even the dinner was fucking delicious. But, although completely stuffed, I came away feeling empty.

A week later Joel telephoned wanting to do it all over again. While inside, I prided myself on my performance, and was flattered at being asked for a repeat, I told him that it didn't really work for me, and that I didn't fancy his boyfriend as much as him. Of course, like most "monogamous" boyfriends worldwide, he arranged to do it the next time Jason was out of town. As planned, Joel picked me up and took me to his house.

As we went through his front door, he pushed me against the wall and kissed me as though desperately hungry. It felt too rough. Ideas flashed into my mind. Is this what I'm giving off? Am I constantly inviting harsh treatment? We seemed to move in one fluid motion from the hall to the bed. He squashed me underneath him with the weight of his solid compact body, holding my arms above my head. Once I was firmly staked by his huge hands, he pressed his lips against mine, and forced his tongue deep inside my mouth. As he pulled it out, he lifted his torso up over me; hovered, then lowered himself down, pressing his crotch heavily onto my face. This felt predictable but at the same time sent a massive spark like rush deep into my stomach, which seemed to massage something in my balls. Fucking lovely! With just one hand, and the heavy weight of his body, he held my wrists. Then he opened his fly and grabbed a hold of his dick. I knew from last time it wasn't going to come out easily, because it was so fucking thick and it had an enormous head. With pure will on his side, he managed to pry it out. And when he did. Jesus! It was warm, and smooth, and smelt incredible. He pressed it up against my nose and in the sockets of my eyes and used the weight of it to bang my face. There was something reassuring about it, which sent part of me mind back into childhood. I understood his teasing so kept my mouth closed but I couldn't help but nuzzle round his shaft, his hair and balls. He couldn't have made me want it/him more. His smell pounded my senses, overriding my consciousness and thoughts. Inside I was confused with pleasure and wholly consumed. Outside I was pure physicality and fantasy, sensual and lost.

Next, his dick prodded my mouth, lifting and teasing my lips, pre-cum sticking and wetting. I wanted so badly to open and swallow every hot, hard, piece of him. He ground his hips, and pushed his dick into my mouth, straight on down, without pausing to the back of my throat. Joel groaned, like an animal and shouted 'Jesus Christ!' I loved this response, and had no mind to stop him. All I wanted was for him to carry on, to keep giving me whatever the fuck he wanted. Pounding and pounding, he forced his dick deeper into my throat. I couldn't breathe and didn't care. So much pain, and yet all I wanted was for him to carry on. While he was distracted, I managed to free one of my hands and tried to control his hammering, but this fuelled his desire and so he got faster, with even more power and aggression. I reached for my own dick and pulled it free from being wrapped, so hard, in cotton and pre-cum, so swollen and desperate and aching. It felt so hard as I stroked, fast and then faster still, as I was taken further into the fantasy/reality of the scene. Now right with him, as far gone and mean. My own excitement allowed me more, to accept more of what he was giving. Now so close myself, I let go of my dick and got my hand around his ass and it was solid, perfect, pumping and fucking loving me. I pulled him in against me harder and more painfully. He felt mighty and elemental, a powerhouse of will. 'Fucking hell, fuck face,' he shouted, then laughed and moaned, getting faster and wilder and crashing and ramming so far in my throat that I wanted to puke, but didn't have the luxury. I had to breathe. 'Oh my god,' were the last real words he spoke. Then directly came a series of involuntary muscle contractions. In a moment of physical bliss, he froze, and a load of cum burst in my mouth with unreal throbbing, it kept on squirting. I shuddered, swallowing as my load burst and I gasped for air. This made me almost choke in his delicious, mind blowing cum. I could smell it and feel it coating my throat. He collapsed on top of me, his torso flattening my face. Joel stayed just where he was for several perfect minutes, slowly sliding his sweaty crotch, spreading his cum over my now slimy face, neck and chest. I was blissed out. It took minutes before he pulled his chunky dick out of my mouth and rose off me. Slowly, I began to have structured thoughts again. He rolled over, paused, then jumped up with a smile and a wink, then gestured some kind of washing action and headed towards the bathroom.

As soon as we were showered he said, 'Do you mind if I take you home now.' I didn't look at him, or respond properly. 'It's just that I've a meeting first thing in the morning. I've got to get a really early start if I want to make the gym beforehand.' Not only did I feel like a woman in a Seventies movie who had just been used by a man, but I was annoyed at myself. I think this was because I'd liked him, but it may have only been because I felt degraded. The sad bit was I wanted him to respect me and worse still cared that he didn't. The most significant thing about the whole experience was that it made me aware that I might need something a little more connected and possibly deeper than the sex I was use to. I was beginning to want respect. It crept up on me, and there it was demanding a voice, and all it took was a certain situation at the right time to make me realize this. So maybe I did want to feel liked by those I had sex with. Possibly, I even wanted to like them too. I sensed trouble. If I wasn't careful, I might start having feelings, become vulnerable, and opening myself up to all kinds of nonsense.

# 10

Sex. I spent a lot of my time doing things that involved looking for, or having it. When it came to this and making money, Josie's and my lives were definitely separate. In her case, there was her love life and then her career. Josie always seemed to be doing something interesting. Sometimes organizing exhibitions, styling fashion shows, writing songs or film scripts, all sorts of things. Whatever she did, it was usually creative. She was so popular that I felt time spent with her had to be earned.

For the last year, Josie had been seeing a woman — her first relationship with a woman — called Maire. She put a lot of time and energy into this. Being together grounded them both to a certain extent, especially because Maire had a daughter. Josie would still meet me after therapy each Friday, and sometimes she'd see me on Tuesdays as well, because I'd begun to see Sky twice a week.

When I began therapy, Sky had suggested I have two sessions a week, but I'd thought it might be too intrusive, not on my time, but my mind. Apparently, the sessions would link more easily and there would be less pressure on the Friday to cram in everything we wanted to cover. The first time I went on a Tuesday I felt uncomfortable, so presumed that it was probably the right thing to do.

There were so few women in my life, but the ones who were affected me so much. Jess had a way of touching my soul before I even knew I possessed one. My mum hurt me as only a mum can. Sky made me cry from understanding, sadness and joy. Josie simply offered me security and solace.

The funny thing was that when I initially had an assessment for treatment I'd asked for a male psychotherapist, preferably one who was gay, and HIV positive. I assumed they'd be able to relate to me more easily. The first one I was assigned was, as requested, a man, but also suggested that my frequent nose blowing was a way of trying to purge myself. I explained that I'd a cold, and that my sinuses were probably aggravated from relentlessly snorting drugs. On day one of our therapy, he used the word *shit*, but it seemed self-conscious and contrived coming from him. I couldn't take him seriously after that and so he didn't get a second chance. After my experience with this prick, I changed my mind about wanting a male therapist. Fortunately, Sky was the next one I auditioned.

Mark-Central-Park-West-Beard came into town in November. He stayed with a friend with whom he had to "sing for his supper", as he called it. It actually meant he felt he had to spend time with his older, wealthy host. A part of me wanted to be with him, but I knew what I'd have to put up with to get there. Namely, I'd have to take drugs to cope with what he'd do to me. We decided to meet in a leather bar that I sometimes went to. It was easy to hang out there without being too wasted and still pick somebody up. No women were allowed and there was a strict dress code: leather, uniform, fetish and no strong smelling after-shave. They allowed a leather jacket and jeans as long as it looked masculine. Ace came with me for company, moral support and accessory. He looked sweet dressed in a pair of chaps, a harness, with a dog collar and leash. It wasn't long before I was drunk and then took some speed, acid and ecstasy: A useful combination for long, nasty sadomasochistic sex. I began to feel a bit too wasted so went upstairs to a dark, quiet corner where people fucked. I sat on a table with my hands on my knees and stared at the ground trying to concentrate on where I was and what I was supposed to be doing. I thought, *okay, you're out of it, what are you going to do?* And my reply was, *take some more speed.* Then a dust ball caught my attention on a beer-sodden walkway to the toilet. It appeared to be made up of bands of rainbow light. As I watched it rose about three feet off the ground, hovered in the air and pulsated. Then it started to weave in and out of itself, folding and unfolding. I realized that it couldn't have been a dust ball, on a wet floor, but must simply just have been the way the colored lights caught the air. This made sense, until I told Ace who burst out laughing. I found him kneeling on the bar showing some leather daddy his ass, trying to convince him that it was naturally smooth and not shaved.

Of course, I ended up letting Mark come home with me where he abused me more than ever. Once he'd exhausted himself, he wanted to go to sleep. I tried to talk to him, because I was still too high to sleep, but he nodded off. Then for the rest of the night I lay with my eyes open watching shadows in the room and the lights made by cars passing on the street below. The next morning we began play fighting. I was used to fighting, it had always been a part of my life. It seemed to me that to win, it took three things. One was to think quickly, even when frightened. Another was to remember moves that worked. Finally, and probably the most importantly, was to be determined. This last device was what I used in this instance. With all my strength, I pinned Mark down. I remember looking into his face, defeated and weak. With every attempt he made to buck me off, I drew more rage from within me, and with it came more strength and more determination to keep him right where he was. There was a moment where I thought he looked genuinely scared and if he wasn't, he was a fool.

'What am I becoming?' I asked Sky.

'What do you think you're becoming?'

'Somebody who fights because he can't express himself.'

'But you did express yourself.'

'Why couldn't I just tell him?'

'You did, using the vocabulary of your relationship.'

'But this isn't how I want to behave.'

'I'm sure he understood you more than you realized.'

'Do you think?' I said, needing her support.

'I'm not condoning violence, but there's no doubt
in my mind that you expressed what you felt very
clearly.'

'The worst thing is I didn't feel bad about what I
did.'

'Maybe you believe you expressed yourself properly.'

'Maybe.'

Even though I was more confused than ever, I had
to admit I didn't feel as though I'd done something
wrong.

'I think maybe you'd had enough. I think that you
might have wanted to end the abuse so you spoke
with violence.'

Sky had handed me another missing piece of the
puzzle. As I left that day I said thank you. I think
she knew what I meant.

# 11

Jess,

Thanks for your letter.

I miss you.

I'm sorry I haven't been more connected with you, but my head is SO messed up. There are times, like now, when I'm tortured by how much I feel. This can't be how everybody else lives. Nobody would be able to do anything practical, like work, eat, do laundry, and definitely not sleep. It's more complex than just feeling happy or sad. That's too basic. I'll try & explain. I HATE SOMETHING. I can't say what, exactly. But it makes me feel such anger. Also, I miss something, but can't tell what it is.

*Still — I pine for this unnamable thing with a
lot of intensity.*

*Please don't ask me to be clearer.*

*Anyway, it's because of all this that my head
is foggy, my direction unclear, & my goal
unknowable . . .*

*I can screen my real self, but I can't replace it.*

*PLEASE BELEIVE THAT I TRY.*

*Paul.*

I felt depressed. This wasn't something I was usually prone to, but this may have been because there
had never been time when I wasn't high. I tried to
decide who or what had brought it on.

'Sky, what is depression?'

'Let me think,' she said and closed her eyes. She
breathed in deep and made a comical *thinking*
expression. 'I see it, as holding something down. I
think maybe it's suppressing emotions or thoughts.'
With this, she made the action with her hands as
though she were pushing something from her chest
to the level of her abdomen. 'As in depress. You
could look at it as a device for holding things in a
place where they don't have to be dealt with.'

I listened with fascination, and I think because of
this she smiled her sweet-honest-but-never-showy

smile. For me Sky had just turned everything on its head. The healing process wasn't instant. It was much more evolutionary. Understanding emerged, and in time, change happened. The key was being aware that I was suppressing my feelings and seeing that there was a way out.

My letter to Jess was cathartic. It also let her know that I was thinking, and by this, that I was trying to get to a place that she knew. A letter from her arrived within days. Knowing Jess, she'd probably sat down and replied with my letter still in her other hand.

*Dearest Paul,*

*Give yourself a rest. You are fighting with the depths.*

*Love,*

*Jessica.*

I thought I knew what she meant, but wasn't sure. Her letter made me even more confused. One feeling I could identify out of the chaotic mess was the all too familiar I-really-can't-deal-with-this-because-it's-an-overwhelming-hum-of-dissatisfaction.

Once when Sky had to cancel our appointment, I met Josie anyway. True to form, she sat patiently and listened. Then as she pulled a spoon out from her mouth — on it the remains of chocolate mousse — she held up her finger to get my attention. Then she waited for her mousse to dissolve and asked,

'Have you ever thought about meditation?'

'What?' This was very new to me, so much so, that I wasn't quite sure what she'd said.

'Transcendental meditation.' When she didn't get a reply, and registered my blank expression. 'Do you know what it is?'

'Do I?' I asked with a mutter.

'I don't know,' she said, and squeezed my nose. 'You twit. It's called TM for short.'

'Good! I thought it a bit of a mouthful, and not the kind I usually like.'

'Double twit,' she said. 'And Tres Gay.'

'*Mucho* Gay, please. Don't French me.'

'I wouldn't dream of it.'

'You know what they say. Don't dream it, *be* it.'

Josie rolled her eyes, and carried on despite my rotten jokes. She told me how she'd first come across TM, how she worked it into her life, and what use she thought it had been. I was surprised that she hadn't told me about it before, and when I told her this she reminded me that we hadn't really known each other that long. Regardless, she said she'd look into it, try to find a teacher and get back to me.

Four days later, she phoned. I'd have happily forgotten about our conversation but fortunately, she followed through. This was Josie's way. She gave me the telephone number of a man who had taught a friend of hers. Apparently, he was already expecting a call from me. All I had to do was dial, hold the receiver, and introduce myself. Josie couldn't have made it easier. More for her than for me, I phoned and arranged to visit him. I was told to bring along five white flowers, three pieces of fruit, but not grapefruit, and a white handkerchief. I turned up without these things and told the man that I didn't see why such ceremony was necessary. From what I understood, meditation was a state of mind and body. Why the mysticism? My teacher, a middle-aged man with a long silver perm, looked as guru-like as he possibly could. I was left alone to watch a video while he went about running his business. The video was one man's explanation of TM meta-physics and how everything was intrinsically linked. The camera kept zooming in and out, I guessed for dramatic effect. The man was sweating and for some reason he appeared to want to give his speech, all in one go. This entailed constant stopping to look at notes, repeating certain points, him looking to the side as he tried to remember things he meant to say, and lots of scratching, picking and general fidgeting. When the titles came up and music played the Silver Perm Guru came back into the room and asked me what I thought. Unfortunately I told him the truth.

'You're not interested are you?'

'I am,' I said, but I knew I wasn't a good actor.

'Why did you come? Did Josie drag you here?'

'No. It was her idea, but if it works then I'm all for it.'

'If it works?' he said, sounding appalled.

'It just seems like there's so much surrounding this that I find ridiculous.' For Josie's sake I tried to blame it on myself before he got too upset.

'Maybe you're just not ready for it yet.'

'Yeah, maybe that's it. I could call you another time when I think I'm more ready.' I didn't want to give up so easily, but I couldn't bear anything this man stood for.

'Some people don't seem to appreciate what I'm offering them.' He then proceeded to vent his anger and gave me other examples of similar situations. Inside, I was screaming, *let me out of here you fucking nutty fake.*

133 | Aiden Shaw

'I'm sorry,' I said, while not only biting my tongue, but already having digested it, and passed it out. I thought his doorway and hall would be my salvation. I'd my hand on the front door ready to escape when he asked could he share a cab up the street. He had a captive audience for the next five minutes. As he talked, I could see his long filed nails flailing beside me, followed by flashes of white embroidered muslin. Thankfully he got out, and despite his meditative calm, the door shutting on the taxi was qiuet slam-like. By the time I got home, I felt wound up and twisted out of myself. This was my introduction to TM.

Josie was very good about it all, and laughed as I relayed the story, but she wasn't about to let up that easily. Two days later, she called me again. I was in the bath at the time, so completely naked, which wasn't unusual in itself, but the subject matter of our conversation made me feel a little more self conscious than usual. Josie had already tracked down another teacher, a woman, and was particularly excited because she'd written a book that Josie had read. Her name was Nancy Waters. The downside was Nancy charged two hundred pounds for lessons. I did have a beautiful aunt called Nancy. Also I'd once worked in a restaurant washing dishes and there was a lovely waitress with this name, and so it had good associations for me. Nancy the waitress told me that she thought I was well adjusted. I was surprised that anybody as bright and gorgeous and so comfortable in her skin and surroundings could think this of me. After a few weeks I lost my dish washing job. This happened every time I'd had a legal job. Still, Nancy helped me see that I was only a little bit of what I could be. I lost contact with her, and immediately started hoping that I'd find her again some day.

I telephoned my new teacher, spoke to her and was again told I'd need the same things as before, the flowers and so on. Before I could begin to intimate my doubts about the ceremony, she said,

'Josie told me about the obstacles,' she said with a sassy sounding American accent. 'How should I put it . . .' She paused as she probed for the right statement, 'That you encountered last time.' I was going to say something about being relieved but she carried right on. 'Let me start by explaining what these gifts are for. And you'll have to excuse the mysticism, but they're to give thanks to all the teachers that have ever been, including the Maharishi himself.' There were a few seconds silence before she said, 'Yes?' I pictured her raising her eyebrows and lifting up her chin. I felt it meant, *Are you okay with that?*

'Okay,' I said, which meant nothing really, but also sounded like I'd answered her question.

'Honey,' she said, sounding even more used to gays than I was. 'You don't have to believe in any of this, but you can still learn a technique you might find useful for the rest of your life.'

'Thank you,' I said, which meant, I hear you and agree with your outlook. As far as I could tell, this woman had style, intelligence, and balls. I took her address and arranged to see her four days later.

I called a punter who I could rely upon at times like this when I needed extra money. I saved him for special occasions because servicing him got so complicated. I'd have to use a catheter, but this was only the beginning, he was very particular. With long rubber gloves on, I arranged glass bottles — various sizes — for his "specimen collection". I understood his fantasy as somewhere between a medical examination and your everyday water sports scenario. Guesswork aside, it was difficult not to want to know his motives, intent, and history. Was I the voyeur in this scene or just an assistant? Maybe I was more than either of these. Things that I wouldn't feel comfortable knowing. As though on fast-forward, the muscles in his face got very busy, possibly this fantastical show expressed his thoughts; the constructing process, the pausing, the adding to, and then the swapping this for that etcetera. I really didn't know, because I wasn't invited inside his head. It's even possible that my exclusion was part of his fetish. It didn't matter enough to me to mind either way. Wherever his imagination went, it was all a mystery to me. After all, I was only ever a bystander, possibly a spectator, and at least company.

There was no good reason not to go along with Nancy's more broad-minded attitude of the previous request, and so I decided to buy white roses, and red apples I took a handkerchief from Ace's sexkercheif collection. I was certain he'd never need the one whose color professed the wearer to be looking for mutual masturbation. Not the Ace I knew.

On meeting Nancy, I thought she was the picture of an ideal of mine. She reclined on a sofa opposite me. Her blonde hair was molded into curved shapes, and it nestled behind her Versace medallion earrings. If comfort and glamour were what she wanted to express, she nailed it. Nancy was a widow who appeared to live comfortably, so I guessed teaching just gave her "pin money". I didn't resent her at all. She spoke mainly in anecdotes about herself, her friends — The Beatles — and glamorous — I think she mentioned Sophia Loren — movie stars. None of it impressed me but I liked her for liking her life, herself, her past, and the sound of her own voice. Over the years, I'm certain she charmed each and any host, and was given many luxurious and interesting gifts for simply being Nancy. She appeared to be successful. What I mean by this is that I felt that she was good at life, good at living.

She took me into a tiny closet-like room, in which there was a simple little altar. Nancy performed a ceremony and then gave me my mantra (a two syllable word-like sound). I was told it should never be spoken aloud, ever. To meditate I was supposed to repeat my mantra in my head. She told me to sit down, close my eyes, begin my mantra and left the room. After twenty minutes, she came back in and asked me how I felt. I told her that I felt as though I really got something out of it. I saw Nancy one more time and found that when I meditated with her it felt better.

What I discovered and found strange was that I seemed to have two separate kinds of thoughts, at least within the context of meditation. One was to say my mantra inside my head, but I found that if I did this, I could also day dream or visualize images also. I assumed that this was classed as a thought, and had been told by Nancy that if I found myself doing this, I should simply remind myself of my intention, and go back to my mantra. Alternatively, if I pictured the words of my mantra as I imagined it to be spelt, it seemed to leave less room for spoken words to come into my mind, but also for other images. It seemed silent/internal noise was more powerful/overriding than visual imagery. Until this moment, I'd never notice a difference, let alone which was more potent. Nancy told me that men have a tendency to be aggressive about keeping to their mantra. I'm guessing she was referring to the silent/audio kind. She also maintained that the idea is to let the mantra just be, and the ideal was to let it become delicate, then a mere thread of consciousness, which in turn became a plateau of the unconscious where neither sound nor images exist any longer.

It wasn't long before I could achieve elements of this and I'd drift easily whenever I decided to. Where I went, or what happened to my brain/mind, I don't know. It wasn't sleep, because I'd have no recollection of dreams. Yet, it also wasn't the same as when I'd switched off when on Rohypnol. It was more like I took time out. Sometimes when I came returned from it, I felt as though I'd been dead. Not in a macabre way. I just hadn't been there for twenty minutes. Actually, maybe it would be more precise to give up on attempting metaphors or similes. It was simply, the physiological and psychological thing that happened when meditating. Clearly, I didn't understand it very well.

Sky listened as I told her then she replied with a neutral facial expression — i.e. one I couldn't read — then asked me what I thought of all this. Other friends I told showed little interest and I began to feel that they all saw it as some eccentricity and nothing more. I can see why Josie hadn't offered it to me earlier. There are meant to be definite benefits from meditation, intangible and largely untraceable — as one might expect from something that related to traditional sciences only when forced to. I decided to continue, thinking it a small investment. It took only twenty minutes out of my day, which was only one hundred and forty minutes a week. This seemed a miniscule amount of time compared to all the sad, tired, lonely, depressing and purposeless years I'd spent wearing out the floor, my jokes, my foreskin and my soul in nightclubs around London.

# 12

**Everybody stopped calling me. Well, anybody that I'd**
partied with. I thought it safe to assume I no longer
served a purpose. It was probably best they didn't
call, as it meant I kept a safe distance and wasn't
tempted to join them. I could've done with their
support. Well maybe not *their* support, but a gesture of encouragement would have been nice. What
did I expect? On questioning how much I cared, the
conclusion I came to was: I don't know. During
moments of what felt like strength and enlighten-
ment my conclusion was definite: Not at all. This
had been a reticent realization, not something that
I wanted to own up to. It was like admitting that I'd
been wrong or false, or even that I'd been conned by

myself. What had I got out of my drug-fucked daze? The only things I could think worthwhile were a couple of friends, Ace and Josie. (Jess came way before). My friendship with Josie could weather changes of lifestyle, but if I wasn't careful, Ace — and his loyalty with the drug scene — could easily drift out of my life completely. I knew I didn't want this so made efforts against it.

This is how I ended up in The West End. It was mutual territory of sorts — although I increasingly disliked it. This had crept up on me unaware. One week I was comfortable and used to being the last one asked to leave the pubs there, then a few months later the very same places only served as a reminded of how much time I'd wasted in them — so I thought this a good place to meet Ace. We planned on the Compton Arms pub at seven o'clock. Stupidly I arrived early. This was a habit drummed into me by my mum, which I'd never been able to shake off. Once I'd got a drink from the bar I spoke to a few men I barely recognized. Then I flicked through a gay paper. Finally I watched the surface of my drink far too much, but decided that it was the most interesting thing I did there.

After an hour of waiting, I felt dejected and left. I called Ace; we sorted it out, and arranged to meet again in the same place at nine pm. To preempt too long a wait I sat in a coffee shop first and headed in the pub just on time. Now that I was already familiar with how to kill time in the Compton Arms (like everybody else who went there) I went straight to watching the surface of my drink. Again he didn't show. I felt so miserable, on a superficial level having worn out every pose, stance, attitude and facial expression I'd have once used in such places, but on a deeper level that Ace was slipping away from me and apparently he didn't give a fuck. I could have cried but instead, feeling insulted, deeply lonely and abandoned I left. As I turned off Compton Street onto Brewer Street a beaming, freckly face appeared in front of me. It was Trish, an Australian friend of mine that I used to share a squat with for a couple of months. As usual she was dressed a bit un-London, and had too much flowery perfume on — probably because she hung out with gay men so much — to accentuate her femininity.

'Jesus!' said Trish. 'You were miles away.'

'I'm definitely here I'm sorry to say.'

'Poor love! Everything Trish said sounded as though it ended with an exclamation or question mark. 'Having a bad day are we?'

'Yeah. Ace . . .'

'Say no more!'

'We were meant to meet . . .'

'And he didn't show. If I'd a dollar for every time . . .'

'A dollar?' I burst out laughing. 'You're not Down Under now Trish, get used to it.'

'Ah shut you're mouth yah fucking Pom.'

'Trish, you have such a pretty way with words.'

'Yah. Whatever. Even in dollars, with all the money I'd have from the Ace deal, I could get out of this rat hole of a city. Come on. Let's grab a Tequila.'

'Where?'

'Anywhere, where's there's booozze and bllokess! Straight that is!' she said and nudged me as though on stage, but in the sixteenth century.

Trish may have known that I needed some company or it may have been some kind of quirky luck. Whatever the reason, we ended up really drunk and had a great evening together. Admittedly I'd never go to any of the places she took me again, unless I was two feet wide, really, really loud, and extremely Australian. Despite the places we went, I was glad of her company, as I'd begun to wonder if I'd any friends left.

Eventually Ace phoned about a week later. That was after I'd left four messages on his answer machine, trying hard not to sound whiny. Instead of arranging to meet yet again, I offered to call round to his flat and pick him up.

It was sitting-around-outdoors-weather, so I'd prepared a picnic to take to Hampstead Heath. I knew well enough I'd need to lure Ace with the possibility of sex. Neither the food, or/and my company alone wouldn't be enough of an incentive. After all, we could talk on the phone and he could eat baked beans cold out of a tin — his idea of a balanced meal and his favorite. As I stepped out of my flat I took a deep breath. My memory rushed ahead of my conscious mind. It took hold and placed me somewhere comfortable, very normal yet still exciting. I caught up with myself and acknowledged a thought, a sense, and a smell. It was that of fresh cut grass, sharp and certain.

Now I'm in scorching heat, behind classroom glass, dull noises blur from my teacher's mouth. I'm eight years old, sleepy and not concentrating, barely caring, only half-hearing, and desperately longing for class to end. Then this cut grass smell drifts by my nose on a wisp of air; cooling, carrying feelings of hope, release from this place, stuffed full of tables, oppression and many others bored and waiting and half-hearing. We all know that with the breeze comes freedom, at least some time soon, then when freed I'd be lying, looking up to the sky, surrounded by cut heads of buttercup and daisies.

I just couldn't face the tube and so I caught the bus to Ace's. It was Sunday and so the journey was quite fast. I expected to find him still in bed so had brought round some fresh coffee which I knew he loved. Ace answered the door naked and so hid behind it. Then he ran back to bed, his little bum jiggling.

'You've had your hair cut.' I called after him.

'Yeah, it's my marine look.'

As with any image Ace had, he looked more like a *Pierre et Gilles* touched-up photo with bruised-looking lips, perfect skin and the longest lashes. After a quick shower, he towel-dried his hair, put on a cock ring, pulled on his jeans (without under-wear), and we were off.

We got a cab to the Heath. Ace could afford it and said that he couldn't stand the journey otherwise. As we walked down the path and into the trees, I couldn't help noticing how well Ace looked. He was dressed in faded jeans and a perfectly match-ing jacket, which accentuated the color of his eyes.

'Have you been in the sun?' I said.

'No, I've rented a tanning bed. It's great — it just

slips under the bed. I call it, "No sweat", or
"Convenientan."' I wasn't easily fooled by gay cos-
tumes but Ace looked very sexy. It made me feel
older than I actually was. I hadn't been to a club in
ages — that's in "gay years" — and hadn't done
drugs for a lifetime — that's in "gay lives", and I'd
spent Saturday night preparing a picnic. Had I
retired? Was I really that square? If I didn't stop my
thoughts spiraling, I could end up in a self-pitying-
depression that could cloud even this beautiful
sunshine.

In the middle of an open space of green among
the trees, which Ace referred to as a glade, we
stopped and I put down my rucksack. We laid
down our shirts to lie on. I hadn't brought a blanket; I thought it would've been too much. I'd also
decided not to take all the food out of the bag but
just pick things out, as we wanted them.

My plan was to give Ace space to talk about
whatever he wanted, even if it was about clubs,
drugs or sex. The trouble was this meant we ate in
silence. I began to feel uneasy.

'Did you hear that?' Ace said completely unself-
consciously.

'Hear what?'

'The Blackbird.'

'What! Where?'

'Hang on, wait till it sings again.' We waited, baited breath. 'There! There he is, in the tree there.'

On a low branch quite far away, was a bird, but it was brown.

'Right I see it. If you mean that brown bird there,' I said pointing.

'That's her.'

'He doesn't look very black for a blackbird.'

'It's                        not            a                fella.'

'How did you know?'

'It would be black if it was a fella.'

'How'd you know that shit Ace?'

'I used to be into birds when I was a kid.'

'You're joking?'

'No. I had books and binoculars.'

'Stop it! Now I know you're kidding.'

'I was even a member of a club.'

'I don't believe you.'

'Honestly. Promise you won't tell anyone though.'

'I don't know, it depends if you stand me up again.' As I said this I wished I hadn't. The whole mood changed.

'You couldn't resist it could you?'

'Well, I waited in that stupid pub for ages.'

'Big deal! I was out of my head. The last thing on my mind was hanging out in the Compton Arms.'

'Come on! It wouldn't hurt you to stick to a plan.'

'Get you Miss Prim-and-Proper, like you would have been able to make it six months ago. How quickly things change.'

'I'm not going to feel guilty for not doing drugs.'

'Fine, but don't give me a hard time for doing them.'

'I wasn't, I just . . . '

'I don't want to hear it Paul.'

There was a nasty atmosphere surrounding us now. The sun was shining and the air was fresh but not where we were sitting. All I'd wanted was to hang out with a friend and have nice time. All the ingredients were there, but Ace and I simply hadn't the same things in common anymore. After a silence, I changed the subject by asking about his sex life. Ace and I'd always swapped sex stories but his were always more bizarre.

'I made one of the men,' he said obviously enthusiastic to share the story, 'Pick up another one for a three-way and then got him to pick up another.'

'Bossy Boots. Or Greedy Guts. Knowing you, both.'

'Well! I was on coke so it could have been all

three. Someone's got to organize these things or they never happen.'

'And that would be a crime against humanity,' I teased.

'That's for sure.'

'So what happened?'

'The four of us played around, making sure that I was the centre of attention with every hole filled.'

'It sounds like a circus.'

'More like a freak show. I dread to think what any of them looked like.'

'Who cares?'

'Not me! Anyway, I got bored with two of them, so kept the dirtiest one and sent the others home.'

'Did they go home together?'

'Who cares? Anyway! The one who stayed ended up putting three apples up my ass.'

I burst out laughing. 'Ah! How sweet.'

'I felt like roast pig, so I did.'

'Were they Cox's?'

'No, cooking apples.'

'Not even you . . .' We laughed. 'What did it feel like?'

'Surprisingly comfortable because they weren't going in and out, just sitting there.'

'Waiting to ferment?'

151 | Aiden Shaw

'Who can say? Anyway, meanwhile he could get busy doing other things.'

'Jesus Christ! How practical.'

'The best thing was when they were up there, I put my finger into my bum and I could touch one of them. The sphincter couldn't close around them.'

'I didn't know it *could* close anymore.'

'Me neither,'

'Fantastic. Didn't it hurt at all?'

'I don't know. Possibly? I was so out of it. Oh yeah . . .' He started to root about in his jacket pocket. 'That reminds me. I brought some acid. Do you want some?'

'You know I don't.'

'Go on, loosen up a bit.'

'No, for god's sake, Ace.'

'I was just asking, don't get annoyed.'

'I'm not annoyed, but this is hard enough and I'm loose enough.' This obviously wasn't true and I resented the accusation.

'You're uptight if you ask me.'

'Just because you think everything in life revolves round drugs.'

'No. They do make it more interesting though.'

'More confused you mean.'

'Fuck off Paul, you prick. I suppose you've found Jesus too.'

Before the argument could go any further Ace got up and dusted off.

'I'm going for a walk, see what's here.' He then popped the acid into his mouth and started to walk off.

'See you in a minute,' I said hopefully.

'If I'm lucky I'll be more than a minute.'

Ace headed towards a clump of trees and I didn't see him again that day. I lay for a couple of hours, but as the sun started to lose its heat I headed home. I wasn't sure whether I was angry or sad, and if I was sad, was it for Ace or myself?

# 13

At fourteen years old I was into exercising, being fit and healthy. I was a vegetarian and drank non-fat milk. This was at a time when you couldn't buy it in shops and so my mother had to order it specially from our local farmer, as it was only used to feed pigs. Don't ask me why I did any of this. It wasn't as though I had older role models. The only muscle men I was aware of were in the back of my brother's Marvel and DC comics. In those days most people saw it as freakish and unnatural, to deform your body into such shapes. Regardless, by nineteen I'd begun going to a gymnasium, which is what we called them then, not health clubs or fitness centers. Around this time I realized that I liked the way other boys looked who exercised. As my own body contorted into manhood, I noticed that certain other men treated me nicely. I got a lot of attention. It was a particular kind, sexual. Once I understood it, I enjoyed it, toyed with it, worked it, exploited it, had lots of fun and partied hard with it. Sure enough, as I did, the working-out became more difficult. I partied harder and harder as it became less about celebrating what I was, and more about trying not to notice that I didn't feel good about my life, my body, or myself anymore. Eventually I stopped going to the gym altogether. My self-hatred and sense of failure grew as my body diminished. I started wearing long sleeved shirts, which served a dual purpose for they covered the track marks in both of my arms.

Now, my recent history had to be put aside. All the anger I felt towards others and myself had to rest while I faced the long haul back to the gym. The problem was I hadn't liked certain aspects of it the first time round. I knew that I didn't understand this completely and even hid from myself the little I did. I thought that I might possibly have more ammunition this time round. Although, I wasn't sure of this, it was only a hunch. Nancy had encouraged me to believe in my intuition and said that if I did it would strengthen.

This whole gym-thing like many things I did now, I did by myself. None of my club friends got up before lunchtime and the last thing they would have felt like doing was exercising. It was a big deal for me to try this again. I knew that I hated so many things about it and resented so many people who did it. I talked to Sky about this and got a pep talk off Josie. I even meditated before I went, to try and focus. I was pulling out all the stops. I knew this was going to be difficult.

On my first day back. I wore a tracksuit to cover up my body. My skin was nightclub pale, polka dotted with zits, and I hadn't shaved thinking it hardly worthwhile. The gym was almost empty apart from a couple of familiar faces; one that acknowledged me as if to say, *How the mighty have fallen.* Maybe I was just being paranoid but I knew how nasty people could be, so had to be realistic. Regardless, I worked, I sweated a lot, my eyes became red and irritated. In short I looked as though I might drop at any second. I obviously had to ease into it slowly. At least I'd got this far, I was making a real effort. I'd thought it would all be downhill and that my health would just deteriorate until I died. I blamed so much on being HIV positive. Here I was, fighting back, thinking I possibly had a future. I began to get a little more excited about life. I'd a good reason to get out of bed in the morning and to get into it at night. My sleeping patterns began to normalize due to being so tired from the gym. Again, I'd thought that I'd never be able to sleep without tablets. I'd had so little faith in myself. I'd been giving in. I may have even gone along with it if I'd continued to inject my drugs. The greatest precaution I ever took was to ask if it was good stuff. I could easily have overdosed and not made it to the hospital. Or, I could have vomited and choked in my sleep. It became hard for me to believe that I'd had so little respect for my life. I guess I thought I was going to die anyway, so what the hell.

I told Sky about my frustration and how angry I got at the gym. It took so long to get a good body and it all seemed pointless anyway.

'Am I doing it for myself or for those men?' I asked.

'Who do you think it's for?' Sometimes Sky was so predictable. I felt I could have stayed at home and just thrown questions to and from myself, but the funny thing was, I did find the process beneficial.

'I want to feel good about myself again.'

'This doesn't sound like a problem,' she said.

'No, I guess it's not but I also want men to be attracted to me.'

'Is that a problem?'

'No, well I don't want them just to be attracted to me physically.' I was forming the thoughts as I spoke. Often I thought I wouldn't have had thoughts unless I spoke.

'Why?' she said provoking. 'You are attracted to them in that way aren't you?'

'Yes.' It wasn't the same though was it? That uncomfortable feeling was there again. I went quiet and stared at her silver shoes. What therapist would wear silver shoes? How distracting. I wondered if she was aware of it. 'Do you think about the clothes you wear, do you dress down?' Sometimes I'd be allowed to change the subject and would say that if a subject were important enough it would come up again.

'Dressing down, that reminds me of what you told me about your mother dressing up to go to church.'

Now she was bugging me. I hadn't wanted to carry on the conversation about the gym but I certainly didn't want to talk about my mum.

'It's almost time.' I said as I looked at her watch.

I tried not to quote her, for she would always say, 'We're coming to time.'

The following week, as she had suggested, I was able to link my session with the previous one. I was still thinking about the gym and I did want to go further with it, but I'd needed the weekend to think about it and then conclusion I came to was not to fight her, it just wasted our time.

'Maybe,' I said, thinking why I hated myself for letting my body fall into such disrepair. 'I just want to be liked.'

'So why do you get angry?'

'Because I know that I'm as superficial as everyone else . . . and I don't want to be.' How could I expect anyone to treat me any different than I treat them? It was too hideous. In a twisted way it almost seemed just that I should have done this to myself.

While working out, this anger didn't go away. It was so self-defeating and seemed to sap strength from me. Also, I'd lose motivation. I couldn't channel energy to lift a weight, it seemed to go inwards and make me weak. Sometimes I wouldn't go at all, not able to bear the whole process: the paranoia, the anguish, and the self-derision. Still, I persevered. Maybe it was the Catholic in me, torturing myself and assuming that good would come from pain and suffering. I may have even got off on this, and I may have learned it from my mum. She'd worked so hard to bring up eight children. Did she enjoy the self-inflicted misery? Some of my saddest memories surround her. Things like getting a new pair of gloves for Xmas and being so pleased. They were bought for me from a shop — not home made — and they were mine alone, not passed down from one of my older brothers. They were made of grey wool and beautiful. On the way to school the first day I tripped over on the street, fell and tore my gloves. I never fell over. Why now? Why with my brand new, shop bought gloves on? Why was there such injustice in the world? Why was something so precious, good and lovely was destroyed? Why did it not matter how hard my mum worked to pay for them? Clearly life was abstract and arbitrary in its acts of kindness and cruelty. It was summed up for me there in my fall and then when my gloves tore. I cried so much. Not just for my torn gloves, but because of the realization that nothing mattered. Fuck the god I'd loved so much. Of course my mother sewed them up with PVC patches and she was the savior, but I can still feel a pang of pain thinking about it.

# 14

On a daily basis, I analyzed, — in my own hokey way —
myself, and everybody I met. The trouble was the
more I learnt, the less I felt I knew. I always thought
it would be more useful if the opposite were true:
*the more I learnt, the less I knew I felt.*

Therapy. Friday. Afterwards, I decided to stop off
and get some flowers for Spud who was in respite
at the Lighthouse. I hadn't seen him since the previous winter and heard he was quite sick. After the
last weekend at his flat I'd thought it best I avoid
him. I really didn't know if it was appropriate for
me to visit. I always had to go through a little
debate in my head when someone I knew was in
hospital. Maybe he won't want to see me. Maybe he

won't want to see anybody. More importantly, he may not even want to be seen by anybody, but there again, he might be lonely. My "rule of thumb" was to go and see how I was received. I looked around the flower shop. I didn't want anything too bright and cheerful, it seemed too obvious. I knew how snobby people could get about flowers, so no pretty simple ones. I refused to get lilies, thinking they were a cliché of good taste. I saw some others, long hanging purple ones, called 'Love Lies Bleeding.' I loved the name but thought they might be a bit too somber.

'Having trouble?' said a voice behind me who I assumed was an assistant.

'No,' I grunted, as I assumed it was an assistant who was going to try and harass me into buying something. Then as I acknowledged the words, it registered that the voice sounded nice.

'I'm looking for something for my grandmother,' the voice continued. I turned to see who had bothered me and did a double take. A man stood behind me to my side, obviously trying to catch my eye, and he was fucking adorable.

'Oh,' I said and couldn't help smiling.

'She's had a hysterectomy.' Each time he spoke he kind of bent around and under to catch my full attention. I was surprised and didn't feel embarrassed for he was so lovely. It wasn't just his features, although they were a fine balance of the stuff that I'd dreamed of, but it was his manner; so warm with a speck of a smile on his lips and in his eyes, his cheeks, his chin, and even his forehead. The way he looked at me made my stomach flick, but luckily I was distracted by his obvious awkwardness.

'Oh,' I said again, as I showed the full power of words and my eloquent command of them.

He laughed, I think realizing I was having as much of a problem as he was.

We both stood there. I could have kissed him — had he let me, and if it were proper to do such a thing to complete strangers during the day in flower shops — there and then.

'I'm going to visit her now.' He was doing much better than I was.

'You're so beautiful,' I said with a throat full of phlegm. I repeated it, 'You're so beautiful,' as if to make it clearer, but actually it was to acknowledge that I'd really said it. He seemed to hang onto the sentence as though his life depended on it. Then he sighed as though something was over, as though we had established everything. I didn't know why I'd said it, but I can guess that I'd been waiting and holding that sentence for a very long time. It was born of regret and loss and not allowing myself to give up. I'd fought with too much for too long not to be able to say: 'You're so beautiful.' It worked as a force that pulled us together, as though he knew from my words where I'd been and where I so desperately wanted to go. Again we stood in silence. 'Those are called 'Love Lies Bleeding', your grandmother might like them,' I continued, trying to change the subject.

'Hey, back up a little. It's not everyday somebody calls me beautiful. I noticed you as I parked and couldn't believe my luck when you came in here.' Could he be talking about me? Had he noticed me outside the shop? I didn't look good and I didn't feel sexy. It was cold, and I was so wrapped up that only a bit of my face was showing. I even had a cap on, and so couldn't believe what he had said. I'd even have distrusted him but for the way he expressed himself, so carefully. A careful that comes from experience; not contrived or sly. 'Are you busy?'

'No, never,' I said. 'I'm just going to visit a friend at the hospital.'

'Would you like a lift?'

'It's only a block.' I couldn't leave this here, there

had to be more. 'Maybe we could meet in the café when you've finished your visit.'

'I'd love to. Which Café?'

'At the Lighthouse.'

'Okay.' Thank god he knew what the Lighthouse was. 'How long will you be?'

'It's hard to tell, I'm not sure what state he is in really.'

'Oh, I'm sorry, I hope he's okay.'

'Yeah, I'll see soon enough. If I'm going to be a long time I'll pop down and tell you.'

So the arrangement had been made. I bought my flowers — orange roses — and found Spud asleep. Apparently he was on Valium and Morphine so there was no point in waiting around. I wrote him a note and left it on the flowers asking him to call if he felt up to it. I sat with him a few minutes. He was wasting and only vaguely looked like the man I'd known. I couldn't help thinking about how people came in and out of my life. I took hold of his hand. It was so frail. I left the ward feeling conscious of how I was meant to be behaving and even how I should be responding. As often, my self-consciousness outweighed my original feelings.

When I arrived at the café my man was already there. I must have been longer than I'd thought.

'How is he?'

I shrugged in response and was already thinking that my date was even more handsome than I remembered.

'Let me just get a bottle of water.' My mouth was suddenly very dry. 'Would you like anything?'

'Yes, your name.'

'Oh sorry, it's Paul.' I was at least sure of that. 'And you?'

'Keenan Cochrane.' It always seemed to add an air of self-confidence when people introduced themselves with their surname. It took me by surprise. I thought maybe it was unnecessary but remembered that Americans did seem to have a tendency to do this. Whatever. I thought I would allow him to get away with it. At least it wasn't confused or insecure.

While I was at the counter getting served, I thought I'd catch another look at him, just to see what he looked like from a distance. He was watching me and was going to look away, but smiled. It seemed like I could feel that smile deep within me. I knew on my return to the table I'd have to fake being comfortable and charming. Maybe not. Why should I have been taken seriously? What had I to offer?

'So Mister Cochrane,' I said as I sat down opposite him. 'That sounds very adult. Are you a school teacher?'

'No, just a bit officious.' He responded very well and looked as though he could have dealt with anything I could have thrown at him.

'So how is he?' he repeated.

'He was asleep.' Feeling my way, I went a little further. 'I could hardly recognize him. He's lost so much weight.' Keenan looked down at his coffee, then returned a look into my eyes, not aggressive but very definite. 'Are you close to him?'

'Close enough to hate it all.'

'Always close enough to hate it all.' This man really seemed to know what I was talking about.

Our conversation had already broken rules. To talk about something we cared about was not usual. Although it was becoming more acceptable as everyone had to face these things everyday.

'He has pneumonia, who knows?'

'Listen, this is just a guess but I think you could do with someone being really nice to you. What do you say?'

'Sounds good to me. Do you know anyone?'

'Yes I do and he'd like to take you out for dinner tonight. If you're not busy.'

'Let me think.' I waited a few seconds with a look of concentration on my face. 'I think I'm free. Yes, I'm almost sure of it. Is this friend of yours okay though?'

'You'll have to see for yourself. I think he'd like you though. He's a friend of my grandmother.' I couldn't help laughing. I felt comfortable playing in this way and he responded so well. Our date was set and I couldn't wait.

It was already early November and I hadn't seen Ace since "the picnic". We hadn't even spoken on the phone. A distance had grown between us, mainly because we weren't doing the same things anymore. I'd started to go to the cinema more, meet friends for coffee and even go to art galleries. Ace didn't like these things. He found them pretentious. His realm was club-life and he felt uncomfortable doing daytime, or more to the point, non-drug ori-entated things. I knew how he felt for I was still on the edge. If the balance tipped I could be where he was. I felt clumsy and awkward in clubs if I wasn't high. The secret for me was to keep it small, never to meet more than one, at most two, people at a time. I'd always have to be somewhere I could talk without shouting. If I'd to raise my voice, I felt it had to be to say something worth hearing. I didn't want that pressure. For me clubs were so much about being seen, showing off, pretending to be more than I was, which made it difficult to say I'm only 'this', even if 'this' had worth, had depth and was interesting, especially if, like me, you didn't truly believe it.

A date, one to one, with somebody I already felt something for, was my idea of a comfortable ideal social gathering. Keenan booked the restaurant, which was a nice change, because normally I always had to take charge. Another thing I liked was that he chose an unpretentious place, both cozy and romantic. It was called Maggie Jones, just off Kensington High Street (not far from where I lived). The waiters were very "New York", good table manners, casual and hip. It came across as, — *the food speaks for itself,* and it did. You know how it is on a first date, you judge the other person by every single thing that they do. He ordered medallions of Venison with a West Riding sauce (I found his choice, both classic and somehow — call me a freak but — masculine), and because he was so impressed, he made me taste it saying *it was the best meat he'd had in his my mouth in years.* I'd heard the joke before, but appreciated his attempt at being sexy. And personally, I love it when somebody isn't prissy about sharing their fork, because let's be realistic, if the date goes well you'll be sharing more than that. I had their famous Steak and Mango casserole. We had enough red wine to make even me be too open about how I was feeling, and then a Muscat desert wine, always a winner with me. If you're not already getting the picture, the meal seduced me big time. I'm not saying I'm easy, but get me all satisfied like this and I'm much more persuadable. You know what they say — *The way to man's heart is through his stomach.* Or as Ace would say, *No darling, it's through his ass.*

To jump forward slightly, we kissed good night and it was as it should be. Gallantly, he dropped me off. I didn't ask him in, as I don't like to put-out on a first date — if I like them that is — it's more likely you'll be asked out on a second. As opposed to becoming fuck buddies as Americans call them. Anyway, who knows if it was my tactic, or he just liked me, but he did want another date. Of course I accepted and so we saw each other again, and again, and again, and again, and believe it or not again.

# 15

'Pauly?'

*Shit*, I hesitated. 'Hey,' I said feeling awkward.

'It's mum here.'

'I guessed,' I said as though talking to a child.

'Sorry.'

'What for?' Instantly, she brought out the teenager in me, the same one who left home angry and frustrated. I may as well have been back in her kitchen listening to her moan about washing the dishes, while my only concern was looking in the mirror at all my zits.

'I mean . . . of course you knew it was me. *You* called *me*.'

'Actually, I called to speak to Rose.'

'Oh!' she sounded hurt. 'I'm sorry.'

'Why are you sorry?'

'Oh Pauly, I'm sorry . . . I mean . . .' She stopped. I guessed she didn't know what I'd want to hear her say. For a moment I felt something for her.

'Well . . .' I said. Then without sincerity, 'How are you?' It seemed I couldn't shake off my cynical attitude when talking to her.

'I'm good, thanks.'

'And dad?' She must have known I was being false now.

'He's dad. You know how he is.' She sounded too cheery for my liking. It wasn't as though we were on chatting terms. 'His back's acting up as usual.'

'Oh . . . right his back . . . I forgot.'

'I'll tell him you were asking after him though. He'll be pleased about that.' I didn't answer. 'It's nice to hear from you.' There was silence for a about a minute. 'So! What have you been up to?'

'You don't want to know.'

'Well, I don't want to hear the gory details, but I'd like to know if you're okay.' I was surprised by her response. It was more realistic than I'd have antici-pated. What mum would want to hear about the kind of things I got up to?

'There aren't that many at the moment.' My mood

lightened, as I remembered that my life had changed quite a lot since I'd last spoken to her. Also she seemed different.

'I'm sure there are *gory details*,' she said, laughing, and I noticed that it didn't bug me.

'Well, maybe. No, but seriously, things really have changed for me.'

'What do you mean? In what way?' This was the first time I'd had to think back, and lump everything together. For some reason I didn't really want to, because it felt as though it meant I had to justify myself.

'Nothing really, I'm just not as crazy as I was.'

'How's your health?' *Oh, no. Why so soon?*

'Do you really want to know?'

'Well,' she said, and paused. 'Yes.' Somehow in that one word I heard "a mother's" concern.

'Mum. I'm not prepared to lie anymore, not for anyone.'

'Don't worry, Pauly, I know all about it, Rose told me.'

I froze. She already knew. I suddenly felt as though I'd a sense of her pain and her strength. What must it have taken to be able to say that to her son? More to the point, she must have held on to that knowledge and not been able to speak to me.

How cruel had I been?

'Pauly, I know I was stupid. There I've said it.'

'Really?'

'I was losing you . . . I just didn't want any harm to come to you . . .'

'Mum. It's not all about you.'

'I'm sorry.'

I sighed loudly and rolled my eyes.

'And will you stop saying sorry?'

'I didn't want to drive you away . . . But everything I said came out wrong.'

'Right.' I tried to say something more coherent but couldn't, crying noises were all that would have come out.

'Pauly?'

'What?' I said with a tinge of petulance.

'I love you.'

I was speechless. There was no way I was going to give in that easily. It had gone on too long to be sorted in one little phone call.

'Pauly?'

My name grated. I heard her voice and it was desperate and wounded. It was not how I ever wanted my name to sound.

'Pauly?'

'Can I call you back?' I said, stammering slightly,

'I have to think mum.'

This was on a Thursday. I tried to remember everything that had been said, so that on the following morning I knew exactly where I wanted to begin.

'I want to talk about my mum,' I said to Sky. 'I spoke to her last night.'

'How was that?' she said and rested her head at a slight angle, so that one of her ears was further forward than the other. This meant she was ready to listen. I'd seen people do this in railway stations when announcements were made over the loudspeakers. I usually thought it affected but in this context it seemed a part of her job, to act, so I didn't mind. I saw it merely as a language, no more false than saying that she was listening.

'I phoned to speak to my sister Rose. I didn't expect to have to deal with mum.'

'What do you mean deal with?'

'Well somehow the conversation slid off the path and then we were in the middle of talking about the argument. She knew that I was positive, Rose had told her.' I paused.

'How did you feel about Rose telling her?'

'I was a bit shocked, she just came out with it. She said she knew all about it and that she had been angry, but that it was just that parts of my life were hard to accept. She sounded upset. She said she. . . .'

I couldn't finish the sentence. I couldn't say *she loved me*. Sky passed me the box of tissues and I laughed. 'She said she . . .'

It happened again. I gave up. Sky waited a while until I'd stopped blowing my nose and sniffling. I couldn't look up at her. I never could when I cried. I wouldn't like to feel as though I was exploiting my tears as if to say, *Look at me showing all this emotion.* I guess there was no need to look at her. After all, our sessions were meant to be about me. 'The funny thing is I don't feel like it's sorted out. I don't think I want it to just be forgiven. There's something else too. I can't piece it together properly but it's something like: If everything is resolved then my life is over. If I don't have this problem there's no need to carry on. I don't understand it anymore than that but I definitely feel something along those lines.'

Sky looked puzzled. I tried to explain further but ended up just saying the same thing using different words. We sat in silence for a while, presumably both wondering what this could possibly mean. That was how we worked by that point. I would often suggest things to her and she would some-times develop them or let them go. Eventually she took her fingers away from her lips to speak.

'I'm not sure but I'm thinking along the lines of identity.' I hadn't a clue what she was talking about so had to wait for more. 'Something to do with you creating an identity as an individual that she was not a part of. Perhaps you might feel as though you would be losing your identity, your life, if she accepts your life. I don't know, I think it's probably more complicated than that as well. This is some-thing I'm sure we'll come back to.'

What Sky had said left my mind spinning. Confused, but somehow reassured, I left. We had come to time.

When I arrived home there was a letter waiting for me. It was from Jess and read:

*Dearest Paul,*
   *I will be in London next Thursday. I would love to see you. I will be in Westminster Cathedral at ten o'clock.*
*Love Jessica.*

It was rare that Jess came to London. There was a time when she would visit Sister Therese but now it was only ever for a specific art exhibition. Excited at the prospect of seeing her, ideas of things I wanted to talk about streamed through my head. That morning I woke to the purest of November days. Winter was being held off for the time being and the sharp sunlight caught every shape. It gave well-defined angles to buildings and gilded the smallest of twigs. These days seemed so special for they were here for such a short time. I tried to respect this and used them well. I walked all the way from Earl's Court to Victoria. I even went the long way round via Hyde Park. It took me over an hour in all but I wasn't going to miss a second of this day. I set off at eight am, planning to stop for breakfast on the way, so I arrived at Westminster Cathedral at about 9.30.

As I entered the cathedral, again, as always, I was stunned into silence and reverence. The original design was incomplete, but what has been created was so much more. The unfinished ceiling creates a depth, which provokes the internal. Something of heaven has been created. I entered feeling prepared for this, but I obviously wasn't. Thoughts of my childhood came rushing back to me, of confession and Stations of the Cross, mum and I sat close together in a cold, near empty church. This was something we alone shared. Nobody else in the family ever went to extra services, because they didn't have to. This was exactly why I'd liked it, for I'd chosen to go. I would kneel to pray and feel very holy. I'd loved this time for I believed it all. God was there with me, watching and listening. He would make sure no harm came to me or mum. God knew everything that I thought and felt, He knew I was good.

Now I felt sad that this had gone: no more faith in ultimate good, in something that cared beyond all else. Surely this was all I ever wanted since those evenings, from something or someone.

I was sure that I was being watched: the whore walking up the centre of the aisle as though he were welcome. Should I have come in through the back door or begged entrance from people who were better than me? I went right up to the altar, feeling a certain strength that this was where I'd come from. I was allowed to face this god because he at least knew me and must remember my naïve love. I stood and gazed into the pit above me, then feeling self-conscious, I sat down. I chose the front row so that I could easily be found, but right to the side so as not to spoil the view for anyone else. The light drew away quickly from the centre aisle, so I knelt in a half-light. I closed my eyes. This was familiar, the smells and the softened noises. I thought of Josh.

'Let's talk,' he had said, but I never got the chance. I felt less angry at him now than I had been and thought of the way he used to laugh. It used to feel so good making him laugh like that.

I opened my eyes. If I faced forward everything was peaceful and perfectly still. It was still only nine-forty. I'd twenty minutes to wait. I decided to meditate. Again I closed my eyes. I breathed deeply in preparation. I went into it smoothly and quickly with no physical distractions like twitching or scratching. I silently repeated my mantra. There were gaps of time where I was aware of nothing, then softly eased in a notion of Josie, her smile and her first hello.

'I must remember to call Ace,' I said inside my head. 'Keep to my mantra.' I reminded myself, so I did.

I felt someone kneel down beside me. I opened my eyes and there was Jess. I looked at my watch, it was ten already.

'Jess.'

'I didn't want to disturb you, I thought you might be praying,' she whispered, giggling.

'Hardly!' I said, while trying to keep my voice down.

'I saw you from way off and I thought my little boy is kneeling praying to Jesus for being so bad.'

I loved the way she teased me like this, the running joke being that I was her boy. As we spoke I slowly came round from where I'd been. Sometimes it took a while. I felt calm and nice being with Jess.

'I want to light candles at the back. Are you finished? What were you doing? Were you praying?'

'No. I was meditating.'

'What! You've started meditating? When? Why? Tell me all about it!'

'Well, let's go and sort out the candles first.'

At the back, Jess took out some change from her pocket to put in the charity box.

'It's well worth it,' she said with a wink. She lit three candles.

'Why three?' I said.

'Hush. One's for my sweetheart Mary, one's for Saint Therese and one's for my Ange du peche. Do you know what the means?' She grinned.

'Angel or something?'

'Good boy. My angel of sin. You, my little Paul.'

Jess was so sweet to me and made me truly

believe that she cared. We linked arms as we walked down the steps at the entrance. We went to a café and talked for some time. I told her about how and why I'd begun to meditate. This led on to Josie, then how I was spending my time, then on to Keenan. Then I skated over sex and straight on to therapy. I gave a synopsis of what I thought I knew. I'm sure Jess made up a picture of her own, interpreting what I'd said. I walked her back to Victoria station and as we parted she squeezed my hand.

'My sweet boy, you're hands are not sweating.'

'Why should I be nervous?' I said acting cocky.

'Come visit some time and bring Keenan if you like, he sounds lovely.'

'He is.'

Jess got on her train and went back to Brighton. When I got home that day there was a message on the answer phone from my mum. It was rare to have so much worth remembering in one day. The message asked plainly if I would like to go home for Xmas that year. I hadn't done this for ages. I'd trouble with the idea. To start-off with, I'd friends who were closer than my family, and I usually spent it with them. The truth was I usually all ended up having a miserable time wasted in clubs with the nagging thought in the back of my mind; what the fuck am I doing here? Still, in the "real world" there seemed to be so much falseness surrounding Xmas and this was the last thing I needed now. To my mind, the idea of spending it with family was a picture of hell and I didn't want to be a part of it. But it might be nice. It'd been so long since I'd been at home for Xmas. I went back and forward between not wanting to go, and then softening and changing my mind. In the end I decided just to call my mum and see what came out of my mouth during the conversation.

'Hey, mum?'

'Pauly!' She sounded so happy to hear me.

'It's about coming up there, I'd like to see you . . .'

'Why am I expecting a *but* now?'

'You know I don't fit in.'

'Of course you do, you're family.'

'I'm not though really,' I said half sure, and half fishing for reassurance.'

'Why not?'

*Hey*, I thought. *That's my question not yours.* I had to think on my feet.

'I've got nothing in common with anyone anymore.' She was silent. 'I never did really.'

'What! You think just cause you're gay, you have

nothing in common with any of us?'

It was funny hearing her use the G word.

' . . . I'd like to see you, but I can't handle all that Xmas hoo-hah.'

'Oh,' she said, and sounded as though she had no idea what I meant.

'I want to be with my friends,' I said trying to explain. 'And my boyfriend Keenan.'

'Boyfriend! Really. What's does he do for a living?'

Despite the obvious concerns I could have predicted from my mum, I thought to myself. *Am I in some parallel universe where parents' chitchat like club buddies*? If I was, then I was out of step, because I wasn't about to start telling my mum about some man I was seeing.

'Something sensible? What does it matter.'

'Well tell me something. How tall is he?'

'Mum!'

There was silence again. I'd sounded too angry and impatient.

'Okay then, I'll speak to you soon.'

'Pauly, don't go. Listen, why don't you come up the week before Xmas. There will be no fuss. There'll be no fuss, nobody but me and old moany bones.'

She caught me. There was no way out of this one, well not that I could think of on the spot.

'I guess I could.'

'Oh come on Pauly. It will be nice. I still remember all your favorites. Trifle. Home made soda bread. Chicken and biscuits?'

'You had me at Trifle.'

'Lovely!'

'I've just to sort out some things here, and I'll call and let you know my estimated time of arrival.'

'You silly bugger. Is that fancy London talk?'

'No. Just Paul talk.'

So it was agreed. And surprisingly when I hung up I felt okay about the whole thing. Anyway it was a while off yet, just in case I wanted to change my mind. I spoke to Keenan about it all and he was fantastic, as he was proving always to be. He even asked if I would like him to pick me up when I was ready to come home. He suggested that it was probably best that I went up by myself so that my mum and I could have some time alone. He said that he would love to meet her and thought nothing of driving over a hundred miles to rescue me. He was so cute and thoughtful. I agreed, thinking I would much rather have him to look at all the way home than the bleak winter landscape from a train window. I was only going for a weekend but it took a lot of effort mentally. My planned visit was the topic of conversation during most of my following sessions with Sky, although it became clear that we couldn't go any further until after I got back. I got a postcard from Jess about a week after I'd seen her.

*Dearest Paul,*

*It seemed so right to talk to you again. It's as if something we both had to work out has been worked out in our different ways.*

*Remaining yours, Jessica.*

I didn't understand it at all, but I knew that I'd been somewhere else and that now I'd come nearer to Jess again and nearer to myself.

# 16

**I got a phone call from Ace's brother, Declan. I didn't** know him, and hadn't even heard of him before. Apparently Ace had asked him to tell me that he was in hospital. When hearing this I was more shocked than upset. I also had a self-centered thought of *It's getting closer. It* being illness and death. I knew that Ace had been positive for eight or nine years at this point. I also knew that he had the most unhealthy lifestyle of anyone I could think of. He seemed to use up all of his resources all of the time but still he was always so strong. Of course I went through all the usual thoughts about my feelings and constructing ideas of how I should respond and behave. I then deconstructed all this in search of some kind of truth about how I felt. It still all seemed more about me.

*Just go and see how he is*, I thought.

*What's the point?* I replied.

*Because he might need you. He might feel scared.*

*What can I do to help?*

*Just be there. At worst you'll be a distraction.*

*I know this scenario already. Are you going to put yourself through it again?*

*Yes, because this time it's Ace.*

Ace. The idea of him unhappy made me sick. I had to get to him. Flowers seemed too silly. This was real life and all that was really needed was to be with him, and then take it from there.

On that Monday morning London had never seemed so grim. The traffic was heavy, the tube unbearable and nobody seemed to care what I was feeling. Rain drizzled, and dragged down all the filth that sat in the sky. I was sticky and felt grubby. *What the hell am I doing living here?* I thought. *Why do I put up with this shit?* Thoughts like these were barely intense enough to outweigh the despair in my mind already.

Once at the hospital I searched through teams of sick people until I found the right ward and Ace's bed. As I approached it I saw that he was sleeping.

He had tubes coming out from his body with some breathing apparatus next to his mouth. *This can't be him,* I thought. *Ace was tough and vital.* I walked back out into the corridor and cried.

I found my way to the canteen and had to wait about ? of an hour until I was ready again. I knew then that a lot of my emotion was self-pitying but I also knew that it had to be dealt with, and now would be an appropriate time, for Ace's sake.

For the second time I approached Ace's bed. He was lying very still with his head turned towards a window. I went around to be in his field of vision. His eyes were open yet he didn't seem to be awake. Then slowly he began to move his head as though only becoming aware that there was someone beside him.

'Paul,' he said so softly. His lips were dry with white saliva frosting the edges. I bent over and kissed him, then made some space on the bed and hugged him. I felt a rush of emotion, and had to think of ridiculous things to stop myself crying. 'It looks so beautiful out,' he continued and seemed slightly lost in his own thoughts. 'More seems to happen in winter.'

I was used to the way Ace spoke. He was very romantic at times. I always said it had something to do with the amount of drugs we took. He'd answer that it was the reason we took so many drugs. He seemed preoccupied. I'd come across this before when people were very sick, or in pain. Something beyond the window seemed to take his attention away from him and me. 'You look great,' he said, without looking at me, but with the slightest sparkle in his eyes.

'You too,' I said, knowing how dry he could be.

'You bastard,' he said, and smiled. He rolled his eyes and made an O shape with his mouth which I knew meant, *how could you*? I was relieved. Ace was still very much there within the husk on the bed. I'd been frightened that he wouldn't know what was going on. I'd thought of every possible horror imaginable since Declan had phoned.

'How long have you been here?' I said. Then, not waiting for an answer, 'I wish you'd told me earlier.'

'There wasn't time, it all happened so quickly. There was so much shit to deal with. I didn't expect all this now.'

'How do you feel?'

'Top of the world.'

His spirits seemed high enough considering, but there was something else about him, a depth or heaviness. Maybe it was resignation.

'Really, how do you feel?'

'I don't know. Confused?'

'Do you know what's happening? When will you be getting out?'

'They're doing some x-rays of my chest. Blah, blah, blah. I don't get told nothing.'

'Is there anything you want?'

'Yeah, there is, but I can't ask you yet, not till I know more.'

'Ace, tell me? I can always get it now just so you'll have it.'

'No, it's not like that. I'll tell you later.'

'But. . . .'

'Let it rest, Paul. How's things with you and Keenan?'

'Okay! As good as it gets for me. I like him a lot but I don't think there's any future in it. The sex has fizzled out.'

'Well, that's because he's your boyfriend isn't it?'

'Probably.'

'Of course it is darling.'

'I thought he was sure about it all, and that was part of the reason I liked him so much. I hoped things would sort themselves out.'

'What do you want out of it?'

'I don't know, a boyfriend?'

'Come on, you know better than that.'

'I don't know better. The thing is I know he's becoming less sure of us. I don't know if it's impatience or just that he realizes that it's never going to be, you know, normal. I'm a prostitute. He says he doesn't mind but it's not about him, it's about me. I know it affects me and I don't even know if stopping will help.'

'And you're not prepared to try.'

'Something like that. Well, not until I feel like it. I'm hoping that I'll feel like it one day.'

'If anyone is capable of sorting it all out, you are.'

'That's sweet,' I said. 'But not true. I do have some faith. Oh, I don't know.'

'Well I'm glad you came to tell me your problems. I haven't a care in the world.'

'I'm sorry, Ace. I'm a selfish bugger. How long have you been here?'

'About three weeks.'

'Jesus. I wish I'd known earlier.'

'It's good to see you now anyway.'

'Does anybody else know you're here? Has anyone been in?'

'It's funny, you know. I couldn't really think of anyone else I wanted to tell. I don't really feel like seeing anyone. It's not exactly society event of the year. What's even funnier is that I wanted to see Dec my brother, of all people. I haven't seen him in years.'

'What about your mum and dad?'

'Dec said that mum wants to come. She's going to try and make it as soon as she can.'

'Do you want me to tell anyone how to get hold of you?'

'Like who?'

Ace looked at me sincerely, and it was only then that I realized exactly what he was saying. There was nobody else. What the hell was it all about? When it came to it, so many of the people/men we spent time with didn't matter. This was depressing, in that I felt so hopeless, but I wouldn't let it out, not then, not with Ace, although it made me think again about everyone around me.

# 17

It was the beginning of December. The city centre was decorated for Xmas and busy with shoppers. My response; get out of town. I asked Keenan if we could go for a drive into the country. There were things that needed sorting out between him and I, and so this seemed a good opportunity. It was Saturday and Keenan was off work. He had a "normal" job and so the weekend meant more to him. From Earls Court we headed out towards Windsor and drove around country lanes. Then we got out of the car and walked along the side of the Thames. After a while, we stopped and had lunch at some horrid restaurant, one of a chain, styled like an old-fashioned inn. We drove some more, then eventually stopped again beside a field. It was simple, flat and green. Keenan suggested we got out of the car and watch the setting sun. We sat against the bonnet. The air was getting cooler so we appreciated its warmth. I thought of the contrast between the artificiality of the car and the natural field. Then I changed my mind, maybe it was the car that was real and something about the field was unreal. It seemed as though something was instigating these ideas or feelings. The strangest thing about this was that this *something* seemed to have a presence, and I felt it here in this field.

It struck me that I'd had this experience before. A couple of weeks earlier, I'd been in my flat and was taking a bath. I heard a noise and had got spooked by it. So much so, that I got out of the bath with water dripping off me. I'd just cum because I'd been soaping my dick too enthusiastically so my dick was plump. I always feel there's something comical about walking around with a hard on (make of this what you will). I'd let the "noise" get to me so much that I'd to check all the windows to make sure they were closed and then double lock the front door. I spoke to Sky about it. I told her that I didn't believe in spirits and wouldn't until I'd had first hand experience. This was reassuring enough, except it was possible that the first hand experience could happen at any time. I sat in my bathtub feeling scared. I tried to think logically and rationalize about the situation.

Over the last year, clearly I'd been opening myself up to accepting a more emotional and even a more spiritual side of life. Yet, because it was all still unclear, and with very blurred edges (that's if they can be defined), I was in all probability confusing anything intangible/inexplicable, or in the slightest way corporeal, and then grouping them together and at the same time merging them under the label "spirit".

'Your fear,' Sky explained, 'may have more to do with your own aggression. I think maybe you know what there is to be scared of, because you have it within yourself, something terrifying. You heard a noise and read it as an aggressor. I believe we're onto something here that may be quite significant.'

I thought to apply Sky's suggestion to the presence in the field. In all likelihood it was coming from my mind. I couldn't be sure because I couldn't really get a handle on what the presence felt like to begin with. The interesting thing for me about this experience was that one thing had changed; I did know for certain that it didn't scare me. I felt so comfortable I asked Keenan if he minded if I meditated.

'It will only take twenty minutes,' I said apologetically.

'I'll wait in the car,' he said. Then as he looked at me, a thought appeared to click in his head. 'Oh sorry, what am I saying? I'll sit here with you.'

I burst out laughing. He was trying very hard to understand and realized that it might be nicer if we shared the moment. I directed, arranged our seating, as I do, sometimes. I stayed on the bonnet, and asked him to stand in between my legs (facing away). Then, when the 20 minutes were up I asked him to let me know. I closed my eyes and breathed deeply. I could smell the earth and feel the damp. I thought through images of peeling back and entering into something within my mind. This was one process I used as preparation before drifting into meditation. Every now and then I would return to notice my senses responding to my environment, the field, then leave all this again. A thought of the conversation I was intending to have with Keenan drifted into my mind. It seemed clear and simple with a direction and a goal. I let this idea go, feeling confident of it, and continued to drift.

Somehow sitting on the bonnet wrapped around him was perfect for meditation, and I think had something to do with being kept grounded in an emotional/physiological way whilst letting my "whatever" go "wherever" it goes while in a meditative state.

'Twenty minutes have gone,' said Keenan

Most times, I would just guess, when meditating, and then when checking if there was still time left I simply closed my eyes and carried on. Sometimes I would be gone for forty minutes before thinking to check the time. Nancy had told me to stick to the twenty minutes for it was a safety valve to only deal with so much at a time. If someone was with me, on the other hand, I was allowed to go longer. Apparently, Nancy used to meditate for hours when in India with the Maharishi.

'Thanks, Lovely Man,' I said.

I put my arm around him and pulled him closer to me. We hugged. I could smell his breath, the wax on his skin, and the grease in his hair. I started to get a hard-on. I pictured him naked. Sections of his body flashed into my mind, disembodied and theoretical, more Hieronymus Bosch than sexual. By now this was a familiar pattern of psychological visuals. This was how I'd begun to think of Keenan, sexually. Not a good sign. I tried to explain.

'When I'm with you and I hold you, I love the affection.'

'My God, where's this leading? As if I can't tell.'

'Please let me finish. I feel very close to you but there is this block when I think about sex.' I watched him, as I knew Sky watched me.

'Go on. What do you mean by block?'

'When the idea of sex comes into my head, it makes me cringe.'

I took a pause again to see how he was responding. 'It's almost like the idea of having sex with my Grandmother. Don't get me wrong she's hot, but it's just not right, is it?'

Keenan burst out laughing.

'It makes you cringe, that's nice.' I didn't know whether he was nervous, covering his embarrassment or just found it ridiculous, but something did break.

'I can't help it. Believe me. I've never felt surer of anyone. I know I can trust you, which is so important for me, but there is this feeling and I just can't get over it.' Our dialogue had turned into a monologue, and it went on winding round and about. 'I thought therapy would help, and it might, but not overnight. I know it isn't fair to keep you hanging on with no hope of change. The trouble is, now I feel pressured and I'm getting all screwed up about it. After all, this *is* all about me isn't it.'

We laughed, I because of nerves and him probably embarrassment. One thing was clear we were
both relieved to have a break from my ranting on.

Eventually between us, or maybe just to shut me
up, it was agreed that he would look for sex elsewhere. Meanwhile I'd to take my feelings of failure
and try to look positively at it all. Josie said that just
because it didn't work with Keenan, didn't mean I
wasn't capable of loving somebody and having sex
with them. Sky suggested that I was probably trying
to piece the relationship together artificially, make it
work because I thought that Keenan was suitable.
She thought the most obvious explanation was that,
as I was getting closer to Keenan, I found it more difficult to connect the sex and emotion. From the very
beginning I'd been wary of getting too familiar with
him physically, in case I found something I didn't
like or worse still, something I did. So I'd fucked
him without really exploring the other un-ass parts
of his body. I didn't actually know how big his dick
was. He could have had any number of balls, I
wouldn't have been any the wiser. It was as though
I was afraid to face it. I hated this idea. Again it
seemed so superficial or just really fucked-up.

Sky asked me about having sex with punters. Did
I get a hard-on? Yes. Did I find them repulsive? To

a certain extent yes, but this didn't mean that I couldn't be turned on by or have sex with them. So it would follow that if I no longer found Keenan sexy, I would still be able to have sex with him, but I didn't, so it must have been a choice, and not necessarily of my mind.

I pointed out to Sky that it was becoming clear that sex without emotion was unsatisfying, yet sex with emotion was still unattainable. This was something that ran deep inside. Knowing it was there was a little of the battle. All I'd to do then was find out what the barrier was all about. I began to feel less guilty about what was happening between Keenan and me. It felt like a fork in a road with a block at each entrance/exit. I could no longer indulge myself in exploring the world of creative, heartless sex for its own sake. Yet I was some kind of virgin freak unable to even enter the word of connected sex and emotion, unprepared for what love might be.

If I could have chosen in what way and how much I felt about people during my life, and just to make it perfect, to what degree and how long I found them sexually attractive, then I'd be in love and live — with the occasional crazy something or other going on — "happily ever after" with Keenan.

As the Spanish say, *Porque no*? If I could have chosen, he would have been at the top of the list. If only life were that simple. Some people might ask: would you have chosen to love someone like Ace, who you knew was HIV positive, and who lived life precariously as a norm? I would say that I would never invite pain into my life, unless that is; I thought it was worth it. Ace was definitely worth it.

# 18

Sunday afternoon I went to the hospital to see Ace. He'd told me on the phone that that he hadn't wanted to take up all my time. What he didn't realize was that I wasn't going out to pubs or clubs at night, and Keenan had decided to spend less time with me "to get his head together". Therapy took up two mornings a week, the gym three, so I'd two mornings and every afternoon for Ace. It wasn't exactly a full schedule and so spending time with my best friend wasn't demanding time-wise. The evenings I tried to keep free to make money, which meant doing a couple of punters a week, although having to be at home to receive phone calls was a full-time job.

Overall, I'd plenty of time for Ace and ultimately he was a priority.

I had a conversation with him on the following Tuesday, which I thought might be a sign that he was getting dementia. The thing was it made such sense, to me. He explained, 'When I was at home, I would lie in bed looking at the wall. I did it all the time. There's a clean-ish mark on what now appears to be a grubby wall where a picture was. I'd stared at that same spot so often that I could still imagine the picture, in detail. There are clean-ish marks like this all over my bedroom. When my roommate left, I'd asked him to move out, he took all his pictures with him. Actually he took the whole personality of the place with him. I never realized I had so little, interior design wise. Anyway, my point is, I can still see them, not the dust marks left, but the actual pictures. So you see, I don't really have the need to have such things around me anymore.'

'Cool soliloquy. But they're not just for you, are they? Your room and the things in it aren't just about function. They're also about how they make you feel when you look at them. Also they're about self-expression. They reassure, reiterate, and remind you what you are, and others simply understand you by what you choose to have around you Admittedly, it's usually just on an intuitive level, unless they know about such things.'

'A. I don't feel anything about my surroundings. And B. . .' Ace had got increasing pragmatic the more ill he became. Sometimes it seemed quite out of character, but there again his "character" was fluid at the best of times. I think he was trying to put things in order, have some control about anything that was happening to him. s'I don't invite anyone into my room anymore so that's not an issue. And C. As far as being reassured by anything anymore, all I'm reassured about is that none of it is important. Let me explain the world according to a dying freak. It's all about deconstruction.' Ace said the words deconstruction as though it were shouted, but without extra volume.

'In what sense?' I asked.

'It's about getting rid of things that aren't necessary in life.'

'That sounds bleak.'

'It sounds realistic to me. It's why some people say I'm so vile. I'm not nice to people anymore.'

'But it's not necessary to be vile either."

'It's not as though I'm really vile. I've just got rid of the faking, the pretending. It takes energy to be nice or vile, but it takes nothing to be nothing. It's the same with furniture, friends, clothes, and hairdos. You name it. It seems apt that I end up here with nothing familiar around me. My friends have become fewer and fewer until there's only a couple left. Ultimately I die by myself. It ends up being about shitting and eating, hot and cold. It's all very basic, just like a baby. I imagine that even love in the end is more about who's looking after me, helping me function."

'So you end up a hermit in a cave on a mountain.'

'Ah! No, see comfort is still necessary. Not big velvet sofas, but duvets and beds and warmth are essential.'

'So there you are being kept clean, warm and alive.'

'Yes, but the being alive can become less of a comfort too.'

'I see. I know what you mean.'

Then Ace's tone changed from matter of fact, to matter of fact with that sincerity that he had shown the previous time I saw him.

'There's more. This is something very important to me, you can't let me down.'

'I won't . . . well I'm almost sure of it . . . well, I guess it depends on what it is.'

'Paul, the way my life is at the moment isn't much fun. Seriously, look at me. I'm not well. Luckily, my mind is still here. It's the only thing I ever liked about myself. If I lost it . . . well let's just say I'd hate that. I'd hate to be that madman over in bed number nine who causes problems from early in the morning. You wouldn't like to see that. I wouldn't like to see that, but this isn't what I wanted to say. It's only going to get worse. . . .'

I started to cry, and the tears were from the 'hillside', as Sky had put it. I was half-looking up as I saw how sad it was to hear someone I loved say these things to me. I was half looking down as I saw how certain he was of his words and how much love was between us.

'Don't cry, Paul . . . You're so sweet.'

I sat in silence. I stared out of the window. I couldn't look at him. 'Paul you have to be really strong, I need this from you. I'm scared. I don't know how much pain I'm going to have to deal with and I'm scared because I didn't plan this and I don't know what happens next, but this can't go on.'

'What do you mean?'

'There's going to be a time soon when I'll want to stop all this shit.'

'What are you saying?'

'You know what I'm saying. There are a few things I want to do. Letters I want to write, people I want to see, mainly my family.'

'Ace?'

'Paul, come on.'

I wouldn't acknowledge what he wanted, not then, although it was all I thought about for the next few days. I found many excuses for not visiting him after that. I knew that I was going up to the Lancashire to see my mum on the weekend, so I called in on the Thursday night before. Ace seemed to have deteriorated so much. It hardly seemed possible. I felt so annoyed that I hadn't been in earlier.

'How do you feel?'

'Top of the world.'

Ace seemed more down than the previous time I'd seen him. I thought maybe he was pissed off. As with everything in life, I'd assumed it had something to do with me.

'Do you want me to go?'

'No. You Fool. I'm just in so much pain,' he said. 'All the time.'

'Where does it hurt?'

'Everywhere.'

'But that's what pain killers are for.'

'They said I'm on the highest dose allowed.'

'Surely there isn't a highest dose.'

'Of course there is. It becomes too toxic for your body to handle and it . . . kills you.'

'You're joking!'

'Yeah! Hilarious isn't it? I should be on TV. Jesus it's all . . .'

'All what?'

'Fucking pointless! Excuse me Sir, could you show me the fire exit please? This is an emergency after all. Isn't it?'

I'd no answer for this. I couldn't see the point of life at the best of times, so hadn't a clue in this case. I tried to lighten the conversation slightly.

'Has your mother been in?'

'Not yet.'

'Do you know when she's coming?'

'No. I haven't heard.' I felt a twist of my heart as I realized what might be going on. Maybe she didn't want to see him. 'She's very busy. My sister's gone on some course with work and had to leave her kids with mum.'

I didn't dare push it any further. I couldn't bear to imagine how painful that might have been to Ace. How alone was he? Apart from his brother Declan, nobody in his family had visited him. He told me that he wasn't too bothered about seeing most of them but he was looking forward to seeing his mum.

'So, I better be going. I'll be back on Monday. I want to get it over with before Xmas.' I felt like I had to pretend to be against things he and I weren't meant to believe in, like family, or religion — in fact, anything "normal". I felt false and awkward. Was this to be the beginning of lies I thought I'd have to tell Ace to protect him. What from? Why should anybody ever be protected from the truth? I got ready to go.

'Paul, will you think about what I asked you on Monday?' He caught me off-guard and I wasn't able to create any more falseness.

'Ace you know I'd do anything for you.' He smiled, and it was so deeply confusing to see a smile meaning something, which seemed so wrong. Regardless, there was something deeper than my confusion, because I knew that his smile was based on a love that shows itself at times, and it cancels everything else out; fear, selfishness, rules and laws. I understood what he wanted and I knew I would try to be there for him, whatever it took.

'See you Monday then. Thanks, Paul. I quite like you.'

'Ninny! See you on Monday. I'll call you from my mum's.'

I left feeling as though I were still sitting there, still in a moment of hatred of everything that had ever caused pain. I kept carrying this moment; it became just another part of my life, another part of me.

At the weekend, I took the train up to Preston, then another onto where my mum lived. I read some of the way and slept the rest. In between were the usual distractions of other people making noise and just being there. I hated the journey and felt like I was wasting my time or somehow going back-wards, back to my family, the house where I'd lived and all the things I'd left home to avoid. It didn't seem to make sense, but so little did.

The front of the house looked much the same. I stood and looked at it remembering; photos of me in front of it at different heights, evolving stages of self-awareness and corresponding haircuts, my sis-ters in clothes that embarrassed them now, my brother flexing his boy-muscles when he was into body-building, several of our dogs that we'd always named shrimp as each one got run over by cars and was replaced. Ah, the memories, or at least nostal-gia. Who ever knew the truth about themselves going through the process of growing up? Usually they're too busy living it to look objectively at it, let alone remember and evaluate it. I stepped closer. So many images from my passed rushed to greet me. Now I was twelve years old, hiding behind my mum as she answered the door to the police when they came to investigate my brother crashing my dad's car. God knows how he knew how to drive it, or reach any of the foot controls at thirteen years old. Closer, I reached for the door handle. It may as well been alive. Did it throb? Or was that always its way of greeting me? Do we have a *cellular* memory that knows more than we think we do, no matter how far we believe we've grown beyond and away from our past? The door was open as always. I walked inside as though I were coming home from school, and gave the doorbell a couple of taps. Our code. I closed it behind me. My mother came out of the kitchen where she'd been cooking. I was as home as I'd ever been. Not estranged, not a gay, weird or in anyway different, just her boy home like any other day.

'I'm in the middle of making you some apple crumble.' There was nervousness in her voice that took me by surprise. It wasn't necessary anymore. I was her son Pauly.

'I love your crumble.'

'That's why I made it dear. There's nobody else here but dad.'

'Where is he?'

'He had a meeting down at the church.' This meant he'd gone for a drink. 'Sure he won't be back till whenever.'

She was older, but because she looked so familiar, I couldn't tell how she'd aged. I could still see her as I'd always seen her, but also I saw a woman who was frail, who had problems, who lived in the same fucked up world as I did. When she smiled, I felt she knew the same joys and the same love. I thought all this as I watched her talk and as I answered, but really I was somewhere else. I was still with Ace, still with Sky, still with Keenan. I was with all these people or rather they were all with me. In fact, they were me. I was simply sitting there with my mother and we were talking to each other. It felt nice. We did the things she always did. We drank lots of tea. She showed me clothes she had made, which I knew she didn't do with my other brothers. I was asked about my friends and what I was doing, but not in too much detail. I was shown around the garden. Then as it got dark, her day was ending. We sat down in the living room and the television went on. When I lived at home, I would always find things to do: drawing, painting, anything but watch TV. It always irritated me; it wasn't about my inner world, my desires or my beliefs. I knew that there were good programs on, but there was so much rubbish in between. I never found it relaxing watching people try to sell me things, but my mother seemed to enjoy this, so I wanted to do it with her. She sat in her corner of the settee where everything was at hand: her sewing basket, reading lamp, and table for her coffee. I sat too.

The room was decorated for Xmas. I recognized some of the ornaments on the tree. So many familiar but strange things surrounded me. The strangest of all was the mantelpiece covered with photographs of weddings, babies and cousins. I didn't understand what it was all about. It meant nothing to me. They weren't about friendship, something we earn. I didn't get the connection between all these strangers. Thoughts like these whirled through my head as I sank further into the settee. My mother offered me biscuits. The heat of the room and blur of TV made me switch off to everything around me. All I knew was that I was safe and warm and my mother was kind. She wanted so badly for me to be happy, more importantly for me to be happy with her in my life, and I felt like I was. I was happy to be there, to be a part of my mother's life as much as I could. I could taste biscuit in my mouth, hear the noise of the TV, and vaguely see the white lights on the Xmas tree. I thought of New York, from high above it in a helicopter, of Gregory, and Central Park. I must have leaned onto my mum because I could smell her perfume. It never smelt like anything in particular, just perfume. When I was tiny she used to drench her coat with the scent and it would engulf me, and protect me from everything, and warm me throughout on cold mornings in church. The smell always made me a little sick, but I found it comforting all the same. Then I could feel the soft wool of her cardigan and her warmth against my face. She breathed in and out. I don't know how long this lasted. How many downers had I taken, trying to recreate this, the security of sleep?

I woke with a blanket over me. It was quiet. My mother had gone to bed, but the lights on the tree still shone. They seemed to ignite synaptic sparks of good thoughts surrounding Xmas but also tease out buried feelings from somewhere deep within me that acknowledged excitement about presents and chocolate and cake. What had my mum dosed me with? How could just being home make me feel so much? The glimmering specks contained hopes and fantasy and magic. It was Xmas, but not simply the ones that I'd lived, been brought up with. These transcended the reality I knew. Yet, it was just another day when I was reminded of how it was meant to be and how far from where I usually was. I fell asleep again.

# 19

I left the next day. This wasn't so much about avoiding my dad — although admittedly all I did was say morning/goodbye as he headed off to work — and it wasn't because it was all I could endure being "home". The reason why I didn't stay longer was that now Keenan and I weren't seeing each other, I had no car ride and so had to catch the train back to London. In itself this wasn't the reason either, but the fact that the train service from London offered something special on Saturdays and Sundays was. Their deal allowed you to upgrade to first class for just a few extra pounds, and although they announced this deal when the train set off, nobody ever came in from the other section. This meant my journey was at least quieter and child-free. Of course their offer didn't make the land-scape any less bleak, but at least I could order tea without leaving my seat.

It was a long journey, but worthwhile I thought. I felt I'd broken new ground with my mother, but at the same I'd been sucked back into a place I'd been in as a child; safe, comfortable, and loved. There was probably something artificial about it. Perhaps it was just a construct to bridge the gap between us, but what is communication if not only ever this? It's very rare that it's more pure. At least we had something. We knew we loved each other in some way, and that was the important thing. What was funny was, trying to talk made it seem like we did-n't. My mother wasn't a person I would call if I had a problem. I wouldn't ask for her advice. What was she for then? Of all the interesting relationships in my life that could be developed, why did I waste time with her? Why was she so deep inside me?

I went straight to the hospital. Ace had head-phones on and tapping his hand lightly on the bed beside him. I told him about the last two days. He listened, and looked sad, even though I'd made sure I played the whole visit down to just the events.

'You make the train journey sound more interesting than seeing your mum.'

'Maybe it was.'

'Oh, come on Paul I may be near deaths door, but I'm still Ace. And I know you Mister.'

'You know how it is with parents, it doesn't take much for them to have a big effect.'

'I guess so.' I stroked his head. He closed his eyes, purred and then laughed. Then without the slightest warning or lead in he said, 'Sweetheart, there's a book about how to commit suicide. Will you get it for me.' He smiled and added, 'Please!'

My laughter crashed to a halt. 'Really?'

I questioned this because I was so surprised. Had we gone this far? Had we been dealing with this for so long that we had written a book that tells us how to die? How much physical pain had inspired this thing? How much anguish creates such a thing? The scale of what was happening seemed to be clearer to me than ever before. This was an ongoing thing; it was not specific to AIDS, only pain. It reached deep into the heart, and resounded deeper still to everything that we're about. The meaning of living seemed to turn inside out, yet it never seemed clearer. I simply had to do something to help my friend and it was a part of life, like protecting a baby, or calming someone in distress, or offering your hand to the frail and old who fall in the street. It was basic compassion. Very few could refuse this to anyone.

I went home after spending about two hours with Ace. I'd the idea of looking through my addresses to find someone who might know of this book, or even better, might have a copy. I had to be careful who I spoke to about it because, after all, it was a dodgy subject. Many people wouldn't be able to understand. They might think it was for me. I didn't know how worried to be about it. I thought of asking Sky about it but rejected this quickly. If I told her at all, it would have to be well after the event. Even though I wouldn't give any incriminating details like where and when, who and why would probably be the subject of many a therapy session.

I thought of someone to ask about the book. He was a writer who'd been on the front line, demonstrating and documenting it since the concept of "gay" began. His involvement in demonstrations, campaigns, and newspapers was legendary, but now he seemed to have settled on a quiet life of writing gay fiction. I'd once skimmed over an article that he had written relating to suicide. He would know about the book and probably would have read it. I'd about five different numbers for him but I guessed he would be at his London flat on Charring Cross road. I started to call him, but paused. Then I pressed a few numbers on the keypad, stopped, changed my mind and went to make a coffee. Then I began the whole process again. This time I let it ring and didn't have time to change my mind before he picked up.

'Hello, it's Paul, from Earl's Court.'

' . . . How are you?' From his voice I could tell he didn't have a clue who I was.

'You don't know who it is do you?' I said, but not to embarrass him, I continued. 'I came round to your flat. Felix from Adams agency sent me round. You said I could call.'

'Oh, Paul, sorry of course I remember you, how could I forget?'

'I've got a favor to ask you.'

'Well, why don't you pop round and see me? Are you still working for Felix?'

'No, but I'm still working.'

'Oh good, well, why don't you come round this afternoon and we can kill two birds with one stone.'

'Great! I'll look forward to it.' I did find him interesting and he wasn't ugly.

'How about six o'clock? I have dinner at eight. You remember the address?'

'Of course.' Everybody knew his address. 'See you at six then.'

I spent the rest of the day doing nothing in particular apart from shaving, cleaning, doing my hair, and generally making an effort. I always felt as though I was making the best of a bad job when I primped in this way. I arrived at ten to six and had to wait outside his flat until he arrived, which was exactly on time.

'Sorry, have you been waiting long? Am I late?'

'No, I'm early.' I felt awkward.

We went upstairs.

'So how can I help you?' He gave me his full attention.

'I think maybe we should talk about that afterwards.'

'Very good. If you prefer.'

We did the business and I noticed how I enjoyed being touched. It seemed like ages since I'd had sex with Keenan and I hadn't done it for fun since. Sometimes when I was working regularly I would forget to have recreational sex altogether. On a practical level, my orgasms would be used up. I think this made me different to other people my age. I didn't have the same drive to hang round parks, or toilets, or wherever. When I did get round to having sex, it had to be worth it. I expected it to be either very exciting or in some way extreme. I know punter-sex isn't like the real thing, but it did seem to satiate something. I think I missed what Keenan gave me, but could do nothing about this.

After washing cum and each other off our hands, we sat down to have tea and slices of fluffy white bread with homemade jam. He seemed to know how to make the whole event nicer. He gave me the money, a figure he had arrived at which was just more than the going rate.

'And you're not to spend that on anything sensible.' I did find him funny, trying to relate to me. 'So tell me, what is it that you wanted me to help you with?'

'To cut a long story short, I have a friend who wants to die. I remembered that article you wrote last year. I thought maybe you would know something about a book you can get, about suicide.'

There was a pause. Presumably, to sort out in his head what I'd just said. I'd expected this. Then he forged out of it with useful information.

'Yes, I do know of a book, although I don't have a copy. What I do have are photocopies from it and various sources that I found interesting. Of course, I also have the article I wrote. Now it's very hard for me not to ask questions but I know it's none of my business. If on the other hand you want to talk about it, I would be happy to listen.'

'No thanks . . . Not yet . . . At some point, maybe. I'd love to sit down and read your article. I don't know much about it all really. It's just my friend wants to know.'

'Fine, just so you know, you can call me anytime about it.'

'That's really nice of you, thanks.'

He gave me some photocopies, and I left. I went straight home with my bundle, and spent the night under a duvet reading, until I fell asleep.

The whole of the next day, I carried on reading. I became an expert in something I wouldn't have guessed at thinking about a few months earlier. Most of the information came from an American book in which they used the term 'self-deliverance' instead of suicide. I found it creepy for the most part; not because of the subject matter, but for the way it was written. Of course, the book was intended to be read by people who for religious, legal, or moral reasons might find it shocking or ungodly. Nevertheless, there seemed to be a distinct air or manipulation about it. For example, the word 'nar-cotics' was used to refer to drugs administered in hospital, whereas the same drugs administered at home for assisted death were 'easers of pain and suf-fering.' I knew Ace would be interested in talking about this. Ace had an eye for truth and the distor-tion of it. He liked nothing better than to root around a subject to find out what was really going on.

I gave Ace the whole bundle and reminded him to let nobody see him reading it. There was a sec-tion on social aspects of terminal illness, another on laws relating to suicide and assisted suicide, which gave examples of 'self-deliverance'. The first section was irrelevant because we didn't care what anyone else thought. This was between Ace and I, and nobody else. The second was useful only in reminding me that I could get charged with manslaughter. The third seemed like fiction. In each new chapter of this section, it conveniently covered different aspects, living a very one-sided view of events. The dialogue seemed con-trived. Ace and I ended up acting out the short scenes. We put on voices: the wife, the doctor, the son, and so on. We tried to recite bits off by heart, making it up where necessary. We laughed so much that one of the nurses came over to comment on it. She said something that was meant to be funny but meant 'Keep the noise down.' We laughed even more at how predictable her comment was. We eventually quieted down feeling good at our understanding of each other. I sat, happy at this. I knew he felt the same.

Generally, when I visited Ace, I would reel off a list of things I'd done or just things I'd thought about. He would tell me what was going on in the ward and what he had seen on TV. When he was tired or lethargic, he would say he had done nothing and had nothing to say. These were the times I wasn't very good at, just sitting, spending time with him with nothing going on. Thankfully, he usually had the energy to try to make me feel comfortable, even if it was just a simple gesture like a wink. Sometimes, if he had his eyes closed, he would make a funny face or blow a kiss.

The most useful information in the reference material was about the lethal dosages of various drugs. It wasn't as simple as taking loads, because they could make you vomit and then some of the drug would escape. Ways round this were to take travel sickness tablets and have a light snack so that the stomach wasn't empty. There were ways of backing up the overdoses like getting into a cold bath, so that hypothermia or even drowning occurred once consciousness was lost. Another back up was to put a plastic bag over the head, making sure it was tight, then to securely tie it around the neck so that it wouldn't come off. In the book, they suggested using a ribbon. Why a ribbon? Ace decided that his way would be to just inject some smack.

'At least I can enjoy myself on the way. I'd like to go to the very limits and then right off the edge.' (This made sense to me.) '. . . And I want you to be with me.'

'Ah . . .' Suddenly this was all very different.

'Ah what?' said Ace.

*What!* *What!* I thought so loudly it must have showed on my face. 'I mean . . . Sure!' I said, with as much certainty as I could muster. I guess I shouldn't have been shocked. Who else would he want there? Nobody. Of course I'd be the person he asked. Still, was this something I could do? Could I be there with him, see it all, and actually play the role he expected of me as "the best friend"? Couldn't he do it by himself? Probably. Would I let him? I wouldn't want him to die alone. But I wouldn't kill myself and expect somebody to watch, *especially* if they loved me. My fear battled with my reasoning. On top of this, I started to feel guilty about doing the drugs. I had been trying to stay clean. *Although*, I thought, *it would just be a one off*, and *it would show that I didn't have a real problem anymore.* 'Sure, I'll be there Baby,' I said. In body at least. I could be sure of that, or could I? Really I had no idea, and only hoped I wouldn't let him down. My head spun with a feeling of vertigo and I could only assume the precipice at which I stood was bottomless.

# 20

Ace had been claiming sickness benefit and hadn't used it whilst in hospital, so I cashed all his money up to date and went shopping to create the party of all parties, Ace and Paul style. Usually, this would have been fun, even exciting. But it wasn't. The theme I decided would be "picnic", and so set about getting things to decorate his flat. Maybe in the back of my mind I wanted to make it how the one we had in the summer *should* have been. From my art school days I knew of window display shops that sold the most unnecessary things. With the help of a sweet young assistant I pulled out boxes and uncovered things that hadn't seen daylight in years. She asked me what they were for. When I told her it was for a party, she got all giggly and overexcited.

'Oh what fun!'

'Yeah,' I said without rising to the occasion.

'What a lucky child.'

'Actually, he's the same age as me.'

'Oh. How funny. What a laugh. You guys are going to have a blast.'

I ended up buying fake grass to cover the floor, big plastic flowers, rubber frogs and quite small details like life size flies, wasps and spiders. Next I stopped at a fabric shop on Berwick Street and got a couple of yards of red gingham for the picnic blanket. Not far away on Old Compton Street I bought a disco ball. This was going to be our sun. From the huge music shop in Piccadilly Circus I found BBC sound effects of riverbanks and bird-song along with his latest pop favorites. Lastly, from Boots (the pharmacist) adjacent I cleared their stock of cotton wool (for clouds, of course). Now I had to get a cab home with my quarry. The cab driv-er noticed the difficulty I had getting all the stuff in the cab, and looked in his mirror. He must have noticed all the odd things. He laughed.

'Having a party are ya?'

'Yep.' Was I missing the joke?

'Can I come?'

'You wouldn't want to. I'm only organizing it, will look great, but won't be much fun.'

At Ace's, I cleared out and cleaned his living room. Then I unpacked and arranged things a little, but had to stop before it got too late. I still had to do a drug run. I went to Brixton and scored a big lump of marijuana, then on to a mate's in Clapham to get forty pounds worth of Heroin, the back into Soho to get twenty E's, some top quality speed and four grams of coke. I bought enough drugs for about five people, that's what I thought it would take for me to be distracted or disassociated enough to pull this event off successfully. Successful being, I enable and watch Ace's death. God knows how I managed to go ahead with my plan. In who's twisted reality was it okay to be a part of this? I found it weird that my love for Ace gave me the strength. That was unless I'd lost the plot and what I was doing had nothing to do with *love*.

Regardless of these thoughts, and this was just the topmost layer — the stuff I could hear in my head — I eventually finished my drug run and went back to mine, exhausted. I woke around eleven, dropped all the drugs off at Ace's, then went to the supermarket and took great care to get all the mixes for his favorite cocktails.

My intention was to create a space that felt idyllic, with nice tastes and things to look at; somewhere that we felt was at least our version of what the world could be like. The other "real" one would be locked away behind his front door.

Once I had everything at Ace's it took a couple of days to put everything in place. He loved hearing about all the preparation and seemed really excited. It seemed that somehow he'd forgotten what it was all for. Maybe that was because he was so doped up on morphine and valium. It made me wonder if he was capable of making decisions about life and death. My experience of both, is that they help you see through the tedium of physicality, the shit basically and you can actually be honest. So eventually, I decided that I was just looking for excuses not to go through with it.

I dragged myself with unwillingness back to the real issue, how do I get Ace out of hospital, and back to our wonderland. It was actually much easier than I imagined. The night before I'd taken the stuff he wanted at home and left some pretend belongings. Things that looked like his, a couple of crap old magazines I found behind his boiler, an old toothbrush that he used for cleaning small hard to reach places around the bathroom, some really cheap toothpaste, half squeezed into his toilet to look used, some jumpers that he must have had since the Eighties, and a paper bag with six donuts in it (I've no idea why I chose them). I replaced his personal items with the junk, but couldn't help eating half of a donut, for authenticity of course. Then I returned the next day and told the nurse on duty that we were just going down to the café. And we did that, well walked by it on our way to the men's toilet where he took off his dressing gown, arm band, and put on the some clothes I'd brought with me. We did this all in silence, as though we were on a top-secret mission. I thought it over the top, but he insisted on wearing a cap and dark glasses, muttering something about disguise and Jackie O. Then we went to the entrance of the building, through the revolving doors and jumped into a cab. Only when we were inside and several streets away did we see the funny side of it.

As we walked in the front door, I could feel Ace's excitement. He was weak, but somehow full of life too, which I think to some degree was just relief. I told him to wait as I ran ahead and played the BBC soundtrack. Then I called to him to follow. When he saw the room he raised his hands to his mouth. This wasn't for effect, but the most real I'd ever seen Ace behave. He flopped onto his sofa, which was now a grass verge with weeping willow branches hanging overhead.

'Thank you! Thank you! Thank you!' he squealed. He looked so happy that I got lost in the moment, and believed I'd done something so fantastic.

'It was nothing really,' I said with mock modesty.

'The flat should always have been like this,' he said. 'I wouldn't have had to go outside ever.'

'It would be hell to clean.'

'Nonsense!'

'And how would you get fresh men?'

'Oh I don't know, you could get them for me. Who cares about such practicalities? On that note, nature doesn't need cleaning. It cleans itself.'

'This isn't real nature though,' I said.

'It's real enough, rather, it's as real as I need it now.'

'Me too.' I smiled then crossed to him and we hugged. I could hardly feel his, although I know he was being enthusiastic, whereas I had to be careful not to crush him.

I'd bought thirty needles just in case. We started with the E. I'd made sure that they were the kind that made us feel affectionate and loving. After this first injection I was relieved of my fear, doubt, and conscience. Just as good gear should. After our first rush, we just lay quietly feeling gorgeous, with rosy cheeks, and smiles that stretched right around our heads. It took about a quarter of an hour before I suggested that we snort some speed to clean us up a bit. This worked perfectly. Soon I was jumping around in front of Ace making him laugh. He took his make-up out and painted on a face that was half geisha and half his imagination let go. We knew we had plenty of time ahead of us, so I could help him remove it later. He did joke about being found like that, or with a big smile painted on his face. I'd bought rubber noses and ears so these were added to the endless list of looks we thought up. He could be a pig lying with a huge piece of chocolate in his hand, or a dog with a leather harness on with the CD repeating 'Old MacDonald Had A Farm.' Because we were high we went on and on. We laughed so much for so long my stomach really ached. Hours passed by so quickly. At one point, we checked the clock and fifteen hours had passed. The phone rang every now and then, and Ace's answer phone message played. It said that he had gone away for a few days, so messages were left. We continued, up, down, rushing then not, resting and injecting some more. I cried and he laughed, then he cried and I laughed as we remembered what we were doing there, until eventually, it was time.

'I've changed my mind,' he said. 'Really I have.' Then he burst out laughing. 'It's a shame to go when life feels this good.'

'But it doesn't usually does it?'

'Yeah, yeah, yeah, I know. I was only kidding.'

'What, you mean you haven't got AIDS?'

'Not for long.'

Again, we laughed and laughed at how brutal we could be.

'Okay this is it.' We were silent. The CD played a track called 'A Whispering Wind Through Chimes'. I helped Ace with his tourniquet, his arms were so skinny and his veins quite messy by that point. We were really wasted. He put in the needle and made a frown-cum-smile, closed his eyes heavily, then opened them again wide. He fell into himself as his life gave in. He held my hands and pulled me towards him. I collapsed on him, squeezing him tight.

'Ace? Ace?' As if it needed to be said that I loved him. He knew I was there every second of the way.

I lay with him for a little while, shocked. Then as though in slow motion I began to cry. At the same time I squeezed Ace and whimpered. Then, quite suddenly, I let go of him, thinking the whole situation was too gruesome. *Coke*, I thought, as though it were the obvious and correct remedy for what damaged me, *And speed. Pull yourself together.* I mixed them, shot them and left.

I'd planned to go to Josie's for two reasons: So that she would back me up if necessary, and because I thought I might not be able to go through with it all by myself. She had already agreed to help me. As I closed the door of the flat, the click of the latch seemed like the switch going off, no more life. By the time I reached Josie's I was a mess. I was crying and could hardly speak. She took control of the situation.

'Now just nod, so I know what's going on. Did he do the smack? Paul, did he?' I nodded.

Josie put her arms around me and sat me down. 'Listen Paul I'm going to get you a drink and I want you to take some valium. Don't worry, everything's going to be okay.' She went to the kitchen and came back with a vodka. 'Drink this; there's two valium here. I want you to take these to relax. I don't want you to go to sleep. It's best if you calm down first. You've been very brave.' I began to cry more ferociously than before and could hardly breathe.

'Don't worry, Paul, I'm here, everything's going to be all right. I wouldn't lie to you would I? Would I? No, see, now take these.'

I swallowed down the valium and kept on drinking the vodka. I began to retch then held it back.

'Come on Paul, look at me.' She pulled my face around to look at her. 'Look at me. Everything's fine.'

I saw her face and I was distracted and started to quiet down. She pulled me down to lie on her lap and stroked my head.

'You're so kind Josie.'

'Nonsense, it's just part of what I'm here for. I want to do this.'

I remember being confused by what she had meant by this, but had so much else on my mind it just joined the confusion. It was early evening but Josie closed the curtain anyway and put a candle on for light. I began to melt into a softer, more manageable state.

'Josie, I'm so scared that I will not be able to deal with this. I might be haunted.'

'Don't be stupid, this is what he wanted and you proved to him how much you loved him.'

'It's just so confusing. I've been told all my life that this is bad . . . you know . . . that life is sacred.'

'What is more important in life than love?'

I needed to hear that so much. Slowly out of the manic turmoil came twinges of good feelings, which seemed to merge around thoughts of Josie and Ace. After about two hours, I was given some sleeping tablets, and slept.

Even though I woke into a soft haze of valium, I could still feel my anxiety rising. Josie had run a bath for me with nice smelling oils in it. I got in it, washed my hair, had a shave and then lay lifeless for some time, with the bath water cooling. *Surely, I should have felt guiltier about what I'd done to Ace,* I thought, but then I corrected myself, *for* Ace. Presumably, I felt disgusted but I'd no sense of perspective, of propriety, of value, morality or even my own feelings. I wondered what Sky might say. I tried to reason but apprehension was all I could muster.

*I did it for Ace,* was one of the voices in my head. *What? Killed him?* was another.

I was hard on myself that day, but this was common. Usually it had more to do with drug come-downs than anything real. The trouble was though, it always felt real so it still had an effect; it definitely still hurt. It got deep so that it scratched and very likely scarred the foundations from which I tried to work.

With these feelings and a jumble of others, Josie and I caught a cab round to Ace's flat and let ourselves in. As could be expected, the flat didn't look like how I thought I'd left it. Josie held my hand as we entered the mess. There was Ace lying face down on the floor beside the chair where I'd left him. He must have fallen out. The room looked storm-struck and he was covered in vomit.

'Ugh!' I said.

'Did you think it was going to be pretty?'

'No, but I don't remember it looking like this.'

'I wonder why?' said Josie. 'When you told me about the room, I had two pictures in my head, your Renoir meets *Alice in Wonderland* version and one very much like this.'

'Shall I sit him back up in the chair?'

'Maybe it's best not to move him.'

'Right!'

'Also we should get to work quickly in case anybody saw us come in.'

'Right.'

'Paul. Stop saying *right*, wash up the glasses you used, and put anything you think you touched in this black bin liner. Especially the needles. They'll have your blood on them.'

'Right.'

'And wear these,' she said, and handed me some rubber washing up gloves.

I put on them on. They were bright yellow. As we moved silently around the room it struck me as feeling weird having Ace lying there dead. First I collected some glasses and washed them. Then picking my way through the debris I started to dump bottles in the black bag Josie had brought with her. They made quite a racket.

'Err!' came a gurgling noise from Ace.

'Oh my god, Paul! He made a noise.'

We both rushed towards him and crouched down. I took hold of him. He was so light I was able to lift him into the chair with no difficulty. As I did this he came to.

'I don't believe it,' I said. 'The bastard's not dead!'

'Excuse me!' were the first words that came out of his mouth, followed by, 'the *bastard*?'

'Fuck Ace! You scared the shit out of me. You freak!'

'That's a nice way to talk.'

'Oh my god!' said Josie.

'By the way, fabulous gloves you two. Tres fashionable.'

'What . . .?' This question had been so unplanned it didn't have an ending or even a middle.

'It's French,' was his response.

'I know that!' I said, raising my voice.

'Were you planning on going on somewhere special after this?'

'Fuck . . . Ace!'

'I won't dignify that remark,' Ace continued.

'Ace,' said Josie. 'Leave it out for a minute!'

'Vomit,' he said as though on some kind of roll. Then he gestured down his body with his hand. 'Everybody will be wearing it next year.'

'Will you shut the fuck up?' I said. 'I'm serious.'

Ace responded with a cough while simultaneously saying 'Cunt!'

'Wow!' said Josie. 'Quite funny for a dead guy. Only *quite*.'

'Everybody finally sick of fashion?'

'You're relentless,' I said.

'Yeah, you can't keep a good man down,' said Ace. 'Apparently.' He slowed down, and his face began to crumble. 'Well I'm still here.'

'Ace stop.'

'Thanks a bloody lot Paul.'

'Listen you,' said Josie. 'Paul's the best friend you could have. 'Can you begin to imagine what he's been through?'

Ace's eyes started to water.

'It's not just about you Ace' I said.

'I know.' Ace started to cry.

'Hey, hey, hey,' I said. 'Don't cry, please.'

'Yeah,' said Josie everything's going to be okay.'

We all sat for a moment with both Josie and I holding Ace.

'You boys want your heads banging together. What were you thinking!' 'Mum!' said Ace while sniffling. 'He started it.'

'I did not!' I said.

'Stop it both of you. And the pair of you be quiet. Actually, sit here and be nice while I make a cup of tea. How does that sound?'

Ace and I both nodded, and were left more thinking than chatting, both avoiding putting into words the most obvious question in our heads. Did he still want to die? Things were suddenly very different. Did we have to go through it all again? How much more confusing could life get? I felt like dismissing the whole thing and just going away somewhere, away from London, from AIDS, and emotion, as if there was such a place in this world.

When Josie came back with tea Ace told her about the party we'd had. He made it sound a lot of fun. It was nice to see them together. Since I'd stopped doing drugs, it felt easier to see one person at a time. One-on-one, there always seemed to be a more positive attitude. As soon as more people were involved, insecurities, egos, and competition came in to play, let alone occasional personality clashes. I was still being affected by all the valium I'd taken, and so was blurry as to the impact this situation was having on me. Still, I found my head buzzing with questions. Would he want to try again, and if so, how soon? Seeing as though I didn't help much the first time, would he still want me to help? I'd still probably be expected to get all the drugs for him. Could I do this for a second time? There again, if he didn't want to try again, then clearly he hadn't made the right decision to begin with, and I went a long with it. My mind was tripping over itself one thought triggering another, all based on emotion, fear, love and guilt. The thing was I felt relieved that I didn't have to deal with the police or officials of any kind. In the bath at Josie's, I'd decided that I could never do it again, this was actually the same thing; I just hadn't done it yet. I heard one word over and over again in my head and it drowned out all the rest. *No! No! No!* But I *was* coming down off drugs. As usual, I was scared, and the decisions I made weren't necessarily coming from my depths.

'How do you feel Ace?' I said.

'Shaky, sick, funny?'

'I bet,' Josie said.

'Well, Ace it's Thursday morning. You're resurrected, and it's not even Easter. In fact it's only one week before Xmas. How are you going to live it this time?'

Ace looked like he was going to say something so Josie and I were ready to listen. After a short while, nothing had come out. I looked at Josie and she looked at me. As we turned back, his eyes were watery. It seemed as though I'd lost the plot again. What could be going on in his mind? Some people lived their whole lives without ever having to face up to anything more than a change of clothes and Ace sat deciding — life or death. To my eyes, he became a boy, injured and lost. It became clear to me what my role was now.

'Ace . . . we can't do it again. Please. I can't give you a good reason why . . . I just . . .'

'I agree,' said Josie.

'Okay,' was all Ace was able to say.

'How do I . . . I just don't think I'm able.'

'Of course you're not,' said Josie.'

'I don't want you to die.' I couldn't look up and so spoke into my lap. Then, I started to cry also.

'Please don't ask me again. I want you to live as long as possible Baby . . . I'm not done with you yet.'

Ace started laughing through his tears. 'Selfish bastard!' he said.

'I want . . . you to stop hurting . . . But not like this . . . please!' I had to stop. Now it was my turn to be comforted, and they both did this. 'I want . . . this all to stop as much as you . . . but not like this.'

I didn't know where these words had come from but it was from somewhere that was really me, somewhere deep within me and wasn't governed by what anybody thought was right or wrong.

Ace got hold of my chin and lifted it. He knelt up.

'I'm sorry Paul.'

'It's just all so grim.'

Ace smiled while he continued to sniffle. 'I don't want to die either, but I know what I think of you.' His expression engulfed me and I felt some peace finally.

'Look at you,' I said with a change of mood. 'Surrounded by grass and flowers; your Highness, Queen of the fairies.'

Josie laughed, and said, 'The place does look great.'

Now there was silence and beaming faces. 'More tea anybody?' said Josie.

'Yes mum,' I said and got up. 'Listen to this track. It's called A Whispering Wind Through Chimes.'

I sat back down behind Ace with him in between my legs and rubbed his shoulders.

'God that feels good,' he said.

It was decided that Ace would put everything on hold for a while and see how things went. We cleaned up the flat and spent Xmas together on our fantasy riverbank.

Ace died on January tenth. He'd passed out one day while we sat watching a film on TV. I called an ambulance and he was rushed back to hospital. He slipped into a coma and let go one morning while I was asleep. Although I'd been saying good-bye to him for some time, it was no easier when it came. There was no point in thinking how unfair, why so soon? All that stuff. That was just how it was, what we all had to get used to.

# 21

Ace in a box. How fucking not appropriate. Being dead
didn't suit him. He simply wasn't somebody who
should have been dead. There was no way I'd go to
the funeral. Not after how I'd felt at Josh's. Josie told
me that she wanted to go.

'He was one of those people who'd always been
there,' she said. Always been funny, beautiful,
clever and soooo twisted. And I thought he'd
always carry on being there.'

'But he's not here anymore,' I said angrily.

'Baby. I know that, but this is the last chance he'll
be here with us, even if it's just in body. We can say
goodbye.'

'Funerals are fucked.'

'Do you know how many friends of mine have regretted not going to funerals? Trust me, too many. Somehow, they serve a purpose. Listen, don't do it for you, or even for Ace, but please, do it for me.'

Keenan arranged to pick me up after the service. It was good to see him. He didn't bring his new boyfriend. I'd spent so much time with Ace over the last few months I'd neglected seeing Keenan. It had probably been for the best. It had given him necessary space. This was obviously what he wanted-ed. He seemed happier. Now that I had more time for him again, he had less time for me. I wasn't his "number one" anymore. I had to decide if what he had left to offer me after the boyfriend was enough. I did expect a lot from my friends so couldn't make this decision straightaway. I decided that I'd let time give me the answer.

As with Josh's funeral, Ace's was only useful in serving as a focus for my anger. I asked if I could say something during the service. It seemed to me that maybe others hadn't known how good Ace was. It wasn't the most obvious thing about him. I sat alone in my living room listening to songs that reminded me of him. Not knowing where to start, I wrote a list of his qualities. Then I thought if some-body hadn't seen these things in him, it would

253 | Aiden Shaw

seem abstract. I didn't want that. I looked at photos of him. I tried to explain in what way I liked him but this seemed idiosyncratic and self-centered. Maybe I should say something romantic to help people cry. This might come across as being pretentious. It wasn't that I minded people thinking this of me; I just didn't want it to detract from what was meant to be going on. Maybe I didn't know what was really going on.

I felt like saying: 'This is all a bag of shit, this fucking disease, and every sad feeling that has ever been caused by it.'

This would be too disrespectful to his parents, who had made time to come a long way on that very special day. I loved him and he'd been so beautiful to me, but did I just want to hear myself say this? Why should I want to share that with people I didn't care about? Did I simply want them to know how I felt? Had this all been removed from Ace the instant he died? He wasn't going to be there. He didn't care who said what, or even if anybody turned up at all. This was now just about my feelings and their feelings.

I decided not to speak at the service and saw it as a failing. I also decided never to go to another funeral and hoped I would never need to. Josie was with me all the way, which helped. Everything seemed easier with somebody to talk it through with. I'd believed before then that I didn't think unless I spoke, but that definitely wasn't the case with emotions. I felt them whether I spoke about them or not, although it seemed as though I didn't deal with them unless I spoke.

I'd met Ace over seven years before. I was in London for the weekend, having traveled up from Brighton for fun and adventure. Seven years, that was a quarter of my life. What was the point of making new friends? How much longer did I have? How would my illness and eventual death affect the people around me? It's odd living your life and always feeling that bit closer to death than everybody else. Of course, everybody knows they will die but some get a lifetime to prepare for it.

I just had to carry on, go to the gym, meditate, see my therapist, to think of other things to do. I decided to do more prostitution, save up some money and take a holiday. This was a harsh thing to distract myself with, but I needed such a distraction. Working hard takes up a lot of mental energy. I joined an agency in the West End, which had a reputation for being the best. I had a haircut, took a course of tanning beds, made myself look as presentable as possible, and went in for the interview.

'Do you suck?' the man said, sitting in an office which hadn't been decorated since the Seventies. It looked and smelt like everything had an inch of nicotine coating it.

'No.'

'Not even with a condom?'

'No.' This wasn't for safety, I just found it too degrading. My interviewer obviously disapproved.

'That's fine; we need to get these things sorted out now. You don't mind getting sucked?'

'No . . . I mean, no, I don't mind getting sucked.'

'Do you get fucked?'

'No, I'm a top.' I thought I'd better say something encouraging here before he gave up on me altogether.

'So you fuck?'

'That's right.' I knew it didn't sound too good, but I also knew that I looked okay, and I was acting very friendly.

'Do you kiss?'

'No.'

'Have you done this kind of work before?'

'Yes, about five years ago. I did it one summer to pay off my overdraft.' I wanted him to think I'd experience but was still a fresh face. I'd to fill out an application form stating what hobbies I had, and what countries I'd visited. This was meant to show what kind of company I would be if escorting. I knew it was nonsense and most of the customers just wanted sex, but I went along with his silly charade. I think it was also meant to make me think the agency was special or glamorous. I just hoped that he didn't believe it.

I had to get a pager, which I wore on the inside of my trousers, not that I minded people thinking I was a prostitute. I did mind them thinking that I thought I looked like a doctor on call, and they knew better. When working I had to be ready for action at all times. They liked to have their boys available as much as possible. I got plenty of work, the pager seemed to go off whenever I sat down to eat, or bathe, or spend time with friends. I could have 'signed off' whenever I wanted, but those things take up all of life so I'd have never been able to work.

I saved money quickly for I didn't have a wish to spend it. I didn't go out at nighttime and hardly felt like shopping, I just wasn't up to it. At least work seemed to have a purpose. It meant I didn't have to think about getting sex, which could take up all of every day, with the bonus being I made lots of money.

I saw Josie at the Lighthouse as usual. Although I was still going to therapy, I was letting it take a back seat in my life. I'd tried so hard to sort things out, to make things work, thinking that Sky might have the answers, yet all we ever seemed to do was discover more questions. I know she helped me deal with my grieving for Ace, but when looking at the bigger picture — my whole life — it became too vast for me to believe it would ever end. My questions always led to other questions. There seemed to be no end to the layers of damage it seemed I'd experienced. I was prepared to keep at it though, assuming I was unaware of what was happening within me, and that presumably Sky was keeping track of it all.

I got a telephone call one night from a punter. From the conversation we had, I knew he was going to be difficult. With agency work it was hard to turn somebody down just because they sounded dubious, for the agency would lose the money as well. I took a cab. When working at any of the more famous or chic hotels, it was best not to arrive on foot. As usual the receptionists inspected me. I was well used to this and sometimes even asked them if there was a problem. They could only guess what I was there for, even though I felt like I looked and walked and talked like a whore, but they had to put up with it. I knew that at worst all they would do is phone up to the room to check if their guest was expecting me. The agency demanded that I wore a suit when going to the hotels but I never bothered. I could hardly be expected to dress like that all the time just in case I was paged.

The customer was German and looked like every other German customer I'd ever had. All customers from the same country seemed to look alike. He was tall, fair, shaved, big-dicked, sun tanned and seemed very clean looking. I recognized his attitude as "a punter".

'Maybe we can do it again and again, maybe all night.' I could tell that he thought it was completely up to him, that I had no say in what happened. 'Maybe you might enjoy it too.' He was what I expected, over-confident and forceful, if not aggressive. I was a toy, his sex toy. He wanted to be fucked. I had to tie some string around my dick and balls so that the blood would stay in my dick to keep it hard. If somebody else did this with me, I'd hate it. I'd assume they weren't turned on by me. He didn't mind. For him it was more about having an object in his ass. It was something he wanted and could have. He could even have it hard if he wanted it. Apparently. I think these things were more important than the sensation, or at least more of a turn-on. Whenever I said to Sky maybe it was this or that or this, she always said maybe it was all of them. I really didn't know what was going on in his mind. It could have been none of them. Who knows? It may have been a way of relieving tension and sharing his wealth.

I fucked him once. Then he ordered some food. To me this didn't make things any nicer, it just seemed to reiterate: 'This is really civilized and you will enjoy this if I tell you to.' I ate and talked just to kill time. I knew that if he wanted to be fucked again then he would have to pay double. This punter told me all about his family, about his beautiful house, how marvelous his life was. I thought to myself, how many other people in your life simply put up with you for some other reason? It seemed hard to believe that he had one personality that he kept for people he liked, and one for me or other prostitutes. I hoped that I experienced the facade and the "other him" was the real him. Maybe he was lovely, and it was *I* who'd brought with me into the situation the abuse, the disrespect, and hatred. Maybe it was both.

He did want to be fucked again and argued when I told him about the price. With contempt or disgust he phoned the agency to check that I wasn't lying. They backed me up and with a struggle he accepted the price agreed. Then he even asked could we work something out between ourselves. As if after all this, I would still want to collude with him. I explained that I could get into trouble with the agency if I did. When I'd worked at another agency I'd agreed to a deal like this with a punter, then he said that he would tell if I tried to charge him. I did charge him and got the sack. So with the German I said no, I didn't trust him. After all the haggling, the phoning, the checking, and him being quite happy to get me into trouble, he said okay. Again, he suggested that I would probably enjoy fucking him. Sure I'd trust him. By this time, I hated him so much that I had to go to the bathroom and just sit and calm down. I thought to myself: *I could just leave and tell the agency that he was messing me around and wouldn't decide and because he had already phoned they would probably believe me.*

*No. Just do it and get it over with.*

*But I can't.*

*Yes you can. Be strong.*

I'd mentioned to Sky before that I could handle most things in my life when I felt strong. She explained that what I meant was, when I could put up strong enough barriers. This was very different from dealing with things from a position of strength.

There was knocking on the door.

'You're not going to spend all night in there are you?'

*Shut up you mad bastard,* I thought. *I hate you*, I screamed inside my head.

I faked a laugh.

'No, I'll just be a second.'

'We don't want to waste any more time do we? Come along.'

He must be insane, I thought. How can two people understand each other so badly? This seemed scary. Does this happen often in life? It could make me lose faith in communication altogether. 'Come along,' he called knocking continually on the door.

I pushed open the door violently knowing he was behind it. I caught his toe.

'Oh I'm so sorry, I didn't realize you were still right outside.'

He hopped around the room like a cartoon character whose foot had been hit by a mallet. How I wished I'd had a mallet. How pathetic was I? I'd stooped to catch somebody's toe with a door, and then pretended it was an accident. 'I'm so sorry, what can I do to help?'

The punter calmed down in time to be fucked again, crouching on all fours, with his face to one side flattened onto the bed. He reminded me of a wounded animal with its front legs broken. His moans though seemed to have nothing to do with pain, but more with his notion of what somebody being fucked was meant to sound like. There was a mirror to one side of me at head and shoulder height. I could see myself moving back and forward but the bottom half of punter and I was cut off. I smiled to myself, then really smiled — surprised to see myself there (in context), smiling. Then I rolled my eyes as I thought about what I was doing there. I knew he couldn't see me, so started to make faces. All the time he continued his groaning.

'Ah! Ah! Ah!' he said. 'Fuck me! Ah!'

I made a face like a squirrel and even brought my hands up to mimic eating a nut, but they smelled of condoms and ass so I stopped. I carried on with this slow repetitive action until my dick got too sore from being tied up so long.

'You're going to have to cum,' I said.

'Oh, I was just getting relaxed.' I wouldn't have been surprised if he had been daydreaming and had

263 | Aiden Shaw

forgotten I was there. I'd been doing everything within my power to do the same, which I'm sure is an odd thing for the mind to have to deal with, receiving a physical sensation and trying to think of other things that were completely unrelated.

'I can't carry on much longer.' I tried to make it sound as though this was because it was so pleasurable and I was about to cum.

'But we have twenty minutes left.'

I obviously had no choice.

'I'm going to cum . . . oh, ah, I'm coming.' I knew I was no good at faking it, but did my best.

'No, no, not yet.'

'Sorry it's too late.'

When I took my dick out, he checked the condom to see if there was any cum in it. Luckily, there was some pre-cum and lubricant.

'You don't cum much, do you.'

'No not the second time, but it feels just as good.' I pretended that *this* was the issue.

'What about me?' he said, putting on a grotesque face which was meant to be like a sulky little boy.

I jerked him off, although he protested that it wasn't enough. I knew the agency would expect no more of me. I got my money and left, again having to argue about what the agreed figure was.

When I got home, I was completely exhausted. I felt like I'd been kicked around and shat on. The smell of rubber wouldn't wash off my hands. On the way home, I'd bought some chocolate as a treat. I sat and began to eat it, then thought this unhealthy, so stopped.

I wondered how different this punter was from ones I'd done when I was high. Maybe the difference was simply that I hadn't been high. It seemed that I wanted to protect myself from the German, but in fact, I think I'd had to build a stronger wall to do this, so maybe I actually damaged myself more. I certainly tortured myself by staying when I wanted to leave. At least on drugs I didn't care to leave, so maybe that was less hard on myself. The drugs could be seen as another wall. Maybe this drug-wall was a false protection, leaving me susceptible — not being able to tell if I was being affected or not.

*Damn!* My fingers. They were brown; the chocolate had melted as I daydreamed. Now they smelt of chocolate and rubber. Again, I thought, I deserve to eat this, and again fought against this and threw it in the bin. At least I wouldn't have to think about it again. I did lick my fingers, it seemed somehow that I'd already okayed eating this much.

After a bath I enjoyed doing nothing. It seemed justified, and definitely a relief after putting up with such a hideous punter. Then I realized that this punter wasn't a very high standard to measure the quality of my life from. Surely, I should be making the most of my time, making every minute count. How many years had already passed since my diagnosis? It goes so quickly. The funny thing was that most people tended to live life faster, faced with this. How could I slow it down? I could read, but if it's interesting, time races by. If I did something boring or tedious, my time would drag by. I could get up early and watch my clock, counting each hour of the day as it goes by. It would be excruciating, but it would be slow.

At this point I decided that I wanted to go out. I wanted to take some drugs and have sex in the way I used to. I reminded myself that I was creating my life and I'd to have confidence in what I chose to do. My mother, Sky, and my friends had guided me, but I must remember that what I am is partly due to what I have chosen to be. What did I want to do? How did I want to spend my life? Ace had tasted this and he'd enjoyed his freedom, I think, even at the expense of losing his family and people who could not understand him, leaving them behind as he lived. Ace had known he had less time than most. For me there was always a struggle between wanting to live life to the full and just wanting to live. Sky said that she thought that I'd given up drugs to protect my health. This upset me: the idea that I might like myself, might want to protect myself, maybe even respect myself enough to care.

I went into the West End alone, caught the end of the bars and then went on to a club. I took some Ecstasy and danced myself so amazingly high: serotonin, adrenalin, and endorphins, what a heady mix. The music was mine; it had my life in it, my memories and all my dreams. There were people in the club that I hadn't seen since last I was there. Some even seemed to be standing in the same places, but I didn't care. I was there for myself to get what I could out of it. I talked with people I didn't know. I laughed and drank and somebody asked if I'd seen Ace. I told them that he had died and secretly smiled at the thought of the twisted fun we used to have. I felt as though I understood what it was all about; the dying, the drugs, the sex and everything else you feel like you understand when you're high. I danced some more and thought of what I was, and what I'd wanted to be, about lovers I'd never had, and of friends that had given me more than I could ever have wished for.

I looked down from a balcony over the crowd. How could I dislike any of these people, any one of them could have been Ace and probably are to somebody.

The feelings of love and acceptance seemed as real as any I'd ever had. In fact, they seemed more real because at least I knew that the drug was having a physical effect on my body. It was real, whereas usually there was always room for doubt.

I recovered slowly over the next week and continued with more passion towards my goal of going away. I bought my plane ticket two weeks in advance and tried to save up my money. I did as many punters as I could possibly stand and, as usual, just a few more.

# 22

**New York — City glamour, no. Miami — sunny beach, yes!** There were moments during the flight when I thought: *What do you think you're doing? Who do you think you are?* To which I was still too unsure to answer. When I'd been taking drugs, I'd thought that I was in the last phase of my life. However, while sitting on the plane I felt as though I'd options. Of course, they were still within the framework of dying but how soon might be more up to me. Now that I was taking better care of myself, things that had been wrong with me and that I'd attributed to HIV seemed to have gone away. It was clear that my former ill health had more to do with my lifestyle at that time.

As I realized how little hope I'd had I started to cry and so shielding either side of my face with my hands, I looked out of the window. I felt it'd been all I deserved. Why — or so I'd thought — should I have expected anything else, anything better?

Once I'd landed, checked into my hotel, and changed into shorts I headed towards the beach. In a café bar on Ocean Drive close to my hotel I lounged, letting every cliché about sun and breeze coat my senses. They didn't just sit on the surface, but sunk in deep within me. I wasn't going to let this experience slip by like a life misspent. Something deep inside me — like a child — cried, *'That feels nice. Give me more! Please!'* These were treasures, so I tore them out of the space around me. It had been a long time since I'd eaten so well. I was starving, and so collected and buried them deep within to nourish me. I could expect to need the memories to comfort me, some time in the future, possibly soon.

The days and nights passed, and while they did, I dozed off under the setting sun, the gentle sound of the waves affording me a kind of serenity and peace. This place was very nice to me, like a nurse who always had the right kind of smile and made you wonder if it could possibly be real. I'd run along the beach early every morning before the crowds and heat. I'd jumped, splashed, and swam in the sea, made my body use itself for what it was for, for living. So often, even though I'd exercised and spent hours at the gym, I'd felt as though it was all just a waste of time. I wasn't athletic and would see myself doing a piece of writing rather than anything sporty. But, here in South Beach, I became so saturated by the physical world around me, that I hadn't the time or the energy to bother noticing what had happened to me: I'd begun to feel great. After being there a week, I finally began to relax. Whilst sitting on the beach, I gently scratched my itchy feet on the sand and squinted into the sunshine. Then from the blue of the sky and the sea walked a young man. He sat down next to me, all freckled, peachy, and fresh looking. His handshake was sure and sandy as he told me his name was Zack. Couldn't he see the shaky, shambles of a mess in my head? Obviously not. All that he could probably see was a stranger, fit and calm, and somebody I didn't think I was. It was an illusion like everything else I appeared to be, but to others, my illusions came across as what I really was. Zack felt comfortable talking to this person he saw as me, and he seemed to not want to let go. Somehow, we talked about me, and my illness, and my drug problems, and everything else that revolved round me, but the odd thing was that we were actually talking about him. Although the *me-I-my* talk sounded like a day of treading water at therapy, he wrung everything he could out of it. I couldn't refuse or resist him, although I wasn't sure which. I couldn't shake Zack off. I was alone on my trip so I didn't mind the company. Zack was scared and was HIV positive and so young. I wanted to take care of him. Although I was certain of this, I wasn't sure I was able.

The light seemed staged by something clever and showy, the breeze effective and loving. The sounds weren't harsh but comforting, assuring me that I was a part of something whole. I spent the rest of my time in South Beach with Zack, "hanging out" as he called it. We didn't have sex. He was very confused, and in pain, sex was a focus point for some of this, relating to his status. We met in the mornings for breakfast, we walked together, he showed me round, we worked-out together, but when evening came he went home and I went back to my hotel. I spent a lot of time with my windows wide open, reading, thinking or simply breathing the fresh sea air.

Zack was my South Beach companion, whom I couldn't have chosen, not before he sat with me. For once, I wasn't being selfish, no matter how I tried to make it so. By my giving him the company he needed — time, and reassurance — it made me feel useful, kind, and strong. I wasn't used to giving these kinds of things to others.

To him they were treats. I didn't know I possessed them, but they'd always been there just waiting to be recognized. I knew too well a life without them. It all changed for me when he sat down. Zack didn't point anything out to me but as we spoke, I felt a welcoming deep within. I'd a realization of what I was doing, as though I'd been shaken kindly and someone had said, 'Look at what you are.'

'What am I?' I'd have had to ask.

'You're damn fine, that's what you are. You're something you wanted to be.'

I could have pretended not to know what this meant, but that would have been the me who wouldn't admit that things could change, telling me that I couldn't be what I wanted. That me was getting told to hush, instead of shouting down anything that tried to have a voice, no matter how sweet it might be to hear. This voice was rising and it was so different for me to have it inside my head. I'm not saying that it was sure beyond all else, but it was strong enough to hold onto, and wonderful enough to not allow it to peter out. So it sang and it was given lessons by the things that happened around it, the things that gave it a purpose and made it useful. Along with it, all of me was fed these things, and it made me feel like I was growing.

I bought some plain postcards that had no pictures on the front, just squares for the stamps. I found this funny. On Josie's I drew the most basic seascape, not child-like but simple and without any passion. On it, I wrote;

*Dear Josie,*
  *I'm enjoying every second of this place.*
*As you can see from the picture, it's idyllic.*
*Love Paul.*

I also sent one to Jess. I didn't draw on it but wrote;

*Dear Jess,*
  *I think I'm changing.*
*I think it's a good thing.*
*Love me.*

Please.

When I left for my flight home, Zack drove me to the airport and we kissed and hugged good-bye.

'You're welcome to come and stay, any time,' I said.

We both seemed sad to leave each other. He held my hand as I checked in, and squeezed it harder than I think he was aware of. His face scrunched and he shifted around uncomfortably as I said good-bye.

'We will keep in contact won't we?' he said, as though to reassure himself.

'Sure,' I said, completely unsure.

On the plane, I wondered whether if we hadn't both been positive, we would have come together in the same way. I felt we wouldn't have. I wondered how many other people on that plane were considering when their life might end. It was right then that this became something I couldn't forget. Whenever I was in a crowd, or at the gym, I thought to myself, how many of these people know their status, are aware of their T-cell count and are monitoring its rise and fall? How many of these people count their symptoms on every new development? In every situation, my answer was: Too many. What a strange thought to have at a party, or a club, or any fun gathering of friends. Nobody invited it but it came all the same. What was our weapon against it? Was it advanced science, or government funding, or public sympathy? No, it was something that comes from the sick, the dying, and those around them who really care. It was the attempt to understand what was really going on.

# 23

**I got back to London and yes, I felt stronger. I found that** I could be alone more easily and enjoyed just letting the days go by. I was determined not to waste my time, but sometimes just sitting and staring into space felt good, as long I made myself aware that I was doing it because I chose to, not because I couldn't be bothered to do anything else. Therefore, like the cliché of the old people on the park bench, I sat and thought about things that had happened in my life. I tried to kindle warmth from the good times and see the bad times as just part of what had got me this far. It was only in retrospect that I could see it like this. No, I didn't think that it answered the

questions of the universe of how and why. Still, it
helped me accept the shit. Why accept the shit in
life? I don't know. Maybe because there's no point
not to, it's there all the same.

It was only two months later that I started to get
ill. I could no longer work for I had shingles across
my abdomen and back, and so I had to claim sickness benefits. A social worker helped me sort it all
out, which was necessary. I'd have just sat and
waited to die by that point. I knew it was going to
be a continual snowballing of things going wrong,
and I could have given in there and then, but my
social worker was very kind. He made things easier
for me and I think for everybody around me. Josie
liked him. She even thought he was cute. Yeah, so
what? Who needs a cute social worker? Then again
why not? I did think it was ironic that one of the
kindest men I'd ever met was paid to be with me.
God, how often I'd faked a smile for money or an
orgasm for a punter, and so many other things to
myself. There I was being shown faked concern. Of
course, some would say that he really did care, and
that it was what he had chosen to do, and it was
good that he was paid to do something he really
cared about. I was just so aware of how important it
was to me. This was what I found sad. I was both-

ered whether my social worker cared. I needed him to care, needed a man to touch me when I felt so ugly, so scared, and not quite resigned to the situation I was in. To show me that there were people left when my entire facade was gone, all the charm, all the strength, all the sparkle from my eyes, and all the sex appeal I'd ever used to get the things I'd wanted. Josie cared. Jess cared; she traveled every other day to see me in the hospital. She put her own life on hold.

'You've been injured,' said Jess. 'I want to make sure you're all right.'

I couldn't help but notice that she'd said *you're all right*, not *get better*. Jess knew that my body wasn't the only thing about me that was injured. She'd watched as I attempted to connect things that had become disconnected. As I'd tried, I imagined that I had a heart that was aware of my soul and that it had the ability to play a part in my actions, and the ways in which I related to others. Further still, I felt I may not have been a shell who'd gotten it all wrong, who'd made one mistake after another with no idea of plot, or depth, or other people's feelings. Jess gave me a glimpse of all this. What a power to have, what strength to give. I'd seen this in her the first time we'd spoken in that little café in Brighton, years before. I'd seen how she could touch the very life of me, hold it and keep it safe in her heart.

'Jess,' I said gesturing to Josie. 'This is somebody else I love.'

My mouth felt sore and dry but I couldn't help grinning, seeing them both together at the corners of my bed.

'Josie, this is Jess.'

Just eight months after I arrived back from Miami, aged twenty-nine, I died. It was only nine months after Ace and two weeks before the death of James who got my bed five days after me.

Like so many others, I'd just wanted to be able to do as I chose. After all, modern medicine had arrogantly stayed the hand of god since long before I was born. All was curable, or would be one day. Yet, I got sick from having sex. How old-fashioned, how crude, how absurd? "Smart bombs" could pinpoint and destroy a target from opposite sides of the planet, and I died because I had sex.

Regardless, had I found anything worth living for? I could count on one hand the amount of times when I thought, *I'm so lucky to be alive*:

One — In Accrington, the small town where I grew up, aged seven. This one may not count because I was too young to actually realize what was happening. I had yellow jaundice and was kept home from school. All I was allowed to eat was crackers and Lucozade. Even though I came from a family of nine (that included my mum and dad), I often felt very alone. It might have been a gay thing. Who knows? Anyway, I was off school for what seemed like ages in child-years, and god knows how I passed the time. I know that I was supposed to lie on the couch under a blanket. Forgive me if this memory is blurred about the rudiments, because the outcome isn't. One day it poured down with rain, like in Africa on TV, only this was in the north of England. I got out from under my blanket and sat in my mum's chair and I looked out through the polka dot net curtains and I watched it the rain pour. Up until now, I'd only ever seen things, but this rain I watched. And I felt it too. It fed my soul.

Two — In Agadir, Morocco aged twenty. I was on a scooter riding through the countryside on a road scratched out of the mountain and heading for a place literally called Paradise. I was with a wonderful friend, and we laughed and laughed and laughed. We felt so happy. I could feel air pockets whizzing by, refreshingly cool then reassuringly warm. I shouted to my friend as I drove up beside him, our T-shirts flapping in the air. 'How lucky are we?' He looked at me and we laughed again.

Three — In Malibu, California aged twenty-two. In a pick-up truck, with a cowboy, well as real a cowboy as I was ever going to bother finding. The sun bleached the hairs as it burnt the skin on my forearm resting on the open window. The hillsides were brown from a summer of parching. It was so simple, this man had given me pleasure, no upset or lies or making me feel like I wasn't enough. The only demand he'd made was to be allowed to enjoy giving me this.

Three — In South Beach, Miami. Eight months before I died. In the ocean, as I splashed and squawked. I felt free and independent, having escaped the soul-destroying drudgery of my life in London. There wasn't a care in the world that could penetrate such bliss.

Sorry, there weren't even a handful. There weren't many of these times for me and none of them was when I was working. None of these times was when I was high, no matter what combination of special drugs I'd taken, no matter how fabulous a party I was meant to be at. None of these times was when I'd released myself from everything constructed, totally ecstatic. These weren't the times that were special.

It takes all sorts of times to make a life, but when I was a child I wanted so much more. I saw men on the television, and they seemed kind, good, and honest. They were what I wanted, not the pain, anguish and AIDS that accompanied them. It seemed my whole life was about men, for men and because of men. I'd even thought that they were worth dying for. Looking back, I probably knew more as a kid, than I did as an adult. Now I know, in my heart of hearts, true freedom was the thing worth dying for.

My happiness didn't come from succeeding. In fact it didn't come from trying to achieve anything at all. It was when I felt: The sun. The air. The sea. The things around me were life itself. Being part of this life was when I was truly happy. This was when I cared whether I lived or died, but I was so stupid, I went back to prostitution, I went back to men with whom I dealt so badly, to drugs that didn't really fool me at the best of times, to working in rooms where I couldn't see the sky, to a lifestyle I created believing it was about freedom even though it went against so many of my childhood dreams. Fuck! Who cares now?

One — A wonderful Josie who wipes her tears on her sleeve — the girls love it — and she's always been a bit of a kid like that.

Two — The profound Jess — a "power-house" of strength. I LOVE THAT WOMAN! — I never understood exactly what we had, but I knew it was as good as it gets.

Three — Sky. Sky! Sky! Sky! What an amazing woman who did her job of giving me connections to so much in my life. I wish I'd met her ten years before. She might even have had a chance with me.

Four — My sister Rose might cry. I can't be certain, and if she did I can be certain if it would be for me, or the idea that she had a brother that died.

Five — An excuse of a mother who arrived too late and who cared too much in the wrong kind of way, who'll be left with the greatest pain, that of never having really known her child and so wasn't allowed to share in his life and death. She'll have so many questions. She sits and stares, so confused, quite indulgent and sorry in ways I don't admire.

She sits and wonders; *Who are these women?* and *Where are the men?*

Before my death, I couldn't see my mum carrying all that pain. It was too late to explain, and if I hadn't been sick, it would always have been too early. This was cruel of me and cruel of her. My cruelty was out of resignation. Hers was out of fear. I'd hoped that she would get some comfort from a letter I'd asked Jess to write. So many times during two years, she'd started and been able to put me to words. Finally she decided that she wasn't able. At least the idea had given me some peace of mind. My mum was to come to terms with my death in her own way. Jess was not her God, nor her forgiver, and not even her teacher now. It was too late.

Sky came to see me the day before I died. This had upset me more than I expected. I think she was the mum I tried so hard to sort things out with, one who could understand, who could even listen to my graphic stories and want to help me feel good about my life. I'm confident that she'll work it all out, but I bet to this day she thinks of me sometimes and sighs and pulls her smile as she remembers how silly I behaved in front of her.

These women are at my bedside. I never would have guessed that this would be the case. That this would be what the end of my life would be like. There was no sex involved with any of these women and I'd thought that sex was so much in life. I remember thinking it affected everything I did but I guess that world of mine wasn't the whole of my world.

I hadn't even told Keenan I was in hospital. The last time I saw him, his glowing face told me all I needed to know about his life and the love he'd found. I couldn't be a part of that, so I decided to stay away.

My sheets were taken and washed, my bed made up again, my pillows — I mean *the* pillows — fluffed and readied for another day, another death. My flowers that Josie had chosen were thrown into the garbage. Everything that showed I was there, that I'd lived, was taken away. I didn't need the mysticism of a funeral but I did want it to be easiest on everyone concerned. Whether they burn or bury me it's only the physical me that goes. Then there's nothing left apart from *their* memories and *their* feelings, the very things that make up a soul.

Photos will help keep their memories fresh for a while. Until the photos become the memories, like those from childhood, indistinguishable from the photos that proved them. Finally, even these are gone along with all the people who felt their feelings and then I'm truly dead.

If I could live my life again, would I be a prostitute? Would I take the drugs I did? Would I have the sex I had? My answer to all of these questions is no, but that's only if I was able to keep everything I'd learnt from them. Otherwise, I would go through everything again.

Adult film legend **Aiden Shaw** is the author of the
bestselling memoir, *My Undoing: Love in the Thick
of Sex, Drugs, Pornography, and Prostitution* and the
series of novels *Brutal, Wasted,* and *Boundaries.*

Born in London, Shaw made his way to
Hollywood where he was discovered by gay adult
film director and industry sensation Chi Chi La Rue.
Shaw has appeared in more than 50 films earning
him international acclaim, as well as the distinction
of serving as the namesake for *Sex and the City*'s
own Aiden Shaw character. More recently the
author studied gay male subculture in 20th century
literature at Goldsmiths University of London where
he received a Masters Degree in Creative and Life
Writing. Shaw divides his time between London and
the U.S. Visit him online at www.aidenshaw.com.